# THE MYSTERY OF THE DRUNKARDS PATH

JODI ALLEN BRICE

"*T*here will be doughnuts."

My head popped up from the kitchen table and I curled my hands around my coffee mug at the sound of my mom's voice.

"Glazed or jelly-filled?" I narrowed my eyes at my mom, Mildred Agnew, who was trying her best to convince me to go to early church service this morning.

"Both." Mom's lips slid into a smile much like the Cheshire cat. She cracked the oven door and checked on her breakfast casserole. "Come on. It will do you good to go to church."

I rolled my eyes. "I'm not much of a churchgoer. Besides, I stayed up late and I'm tired." I didn't even try to hide my yawn.

Mom shut the oven door and turned to look at me. "Dove, all you do is work at the quilt shop and watch TV when you get home. You need more of a social life. Besides, Dean will be there."

"Dean is my ex." I took a sip of my coffee. "Dean and Samantha Vaughn are dating. So stop trying to match us up."

Dean Gray, the chief of police, was my high school sweet-heart. We had broken up after graduation and I had moved to the big city of New York to pursue my dream of making it big in the children's fashion world. I had succeeded until I let my partner con me. Now I was living back home with my mom in Harland Creek and trying to figure out what I was going to do next.

"Samantha's a lovely girl." Mom nodded and sipped her coffee.

I sat up straight. "You think she's lovely?" My mind raced to come up with a reason not to like Samantha, besides the fact she was dating my boyfriend, er, ex-boyfriend.

"Sure. She's a natural beauty." Mom took another sip. "She dresses nice, too. Why, just last Sunday, she wore the prettiest coral-colored dress with pearls."

I didn't bother to hide my sneer. "I bet she wore matching shoes."

Mom blinked. "How did you know? Did you run into her after church?"

"No. But everyone knows that when you wear a color like coral, you wear a nude shoe. It helps elongate the legs."

"Well, she's got pretty long legs, so I guess it doesn't matter."

I sat up straighter. "I have long legs, too."

Mom set her coffee cup down and came over and patted my cheek. "Of course you do, dear. I guess I'll go get dressed for church if you're not going. It would be a shame for you not to come and show off that beautiful ice-blue colored dress you made. It's simply stunning."

I smiled at the praise. I had gotten tired of watching TV one night, so I gathered up some supplies from Mom's fabric horde and found a bolt of shimmery blue fabric. She told me she bought it a couple of years ago and never did anything with it. So she let me have it.

Within a day I had made, without a pattern, a vintage flared A-line swing dress with sleeves. When I tried it on, it made my startling, blue eyes stand out even more.

If I showed up in that dress at church, I bet no one would be talking about Samantha Vaughn and her coral-colored dress.

Thirty minutes later, I was dressed and in the car with my mom.

"Why is church so early today, anyway?" I covered my yawn with my hand. I should have gotten another cup of coffee before leaving the house.

"Farmer Joe Smith is getting baptized today. Whenever we have a baptism, we do it at eight o'clock and then have breakfast before the pastor preaches." Mom shifted the insulated casserole carrier on her lap. "He usually does a shorter sermon on baptism days."

"Thank God." I murmured.

By the time we were pulling into the church parking lot, my stomach was growling. "This baptism better be quick," I scowled.

I got out first and walked around to take the dish from Mom.

"Just put it in the fellowship hall with the others." Mom spotted Elizabeth Harland and waved to her friend.

I hurried through the back door into the fellowship hall with the dish in my hands. I headed into the kitchen and smiled when I saw the elaborate breakfast spread on the counter. Breakfast casseroles, fresh fruit, coffee cake, and most importantly, donuts. We would be eating good today.

I glanced over my shoulder and pilfered a donut. I had taken only one bite before I heard voices heading my way. Embarrassed at being caught red-handed, I ducked behind a door and tried to stay still.

"I can't believe Pastor John yelled at Eleanor like that. I've never even seen him so much as raise his voice in all the years I've known him." Etta Miller, the church secretary, stepped into the room and placed a platter on the counter. She was the shortest woman I knew, and I bet she wasn't even five feet in height.

I peered through the crack at the hinge and spotted the two ladies that I had known all my life.

"He actually yelled?" Agnes Jackson crossed her arms and studied Etta like she didn't believe her.

"I wouldn't lie, Agnes." Etta lifted her chin and scowled.

"Well, what were they arguing about?"

Etta glanced around and lowered her voice. "Eleanor said she would not give Pastor John any more money to fund our missionaries."

Agnes gasped. "She didn't!"

I carefully took a bite of my donut and chewed while listening intently.

"Yes. And that's when Pastor John went off on her. Said she would be sorry if she didn't pay."

"Huh. I wonder what he meant?" Agnes sighed. "Doesn't matter now. We have to get ready for the baptism. Did you bring the towel?"

"I need to grab it out of the office. I'll meet you at the baptistry." Etta headed out of the room, her footsteps heavy on the floor.

"You can come out, Dove." Agnes swung open the door.

I narrowed my eyes. "How did you know it was me?"

"I heard you chewing. Come with me. If I have to help with this, you do too."

I shoved the rest of the donut in my mouth and chewed as I followed her to the baptistry.

Elizabeth Harland and Pastor John were there conversing with Farmer Smith, who was wearing some jean shorts and a T-shirt.

"You're not going to drown me, are you, Pastor?" Farmer Smith gave him an uncertain look.

Pastor John chuckled. "No. I'm only going to put you in the water and raise you back up."

"This is exciting. This is a day of celebration." Elizabeth smiled.

"Sure is A day to celebrate you getting a bath," Agnes snarled.

"Agnes!" Elizabeth shot her friend a glare.

"Well, it's true. His pigs get bathed more often than he does." Agnes narrowed her eyes at her arch nemesis.

"That's unkind and not very Christian." Elizabeth stated.

Agnes sighed. "Fine. I'm sorry."

Farmer Smith shifted his weight. "I don't know. Maybe I should wait. I can do this another time."

"Look, there's nothing to be worried about." Pastor John clasped his hand on the man's shoulder.

"What if I slip and fall and hit my head? What if you can't pull me back out of the water? What if the water's cold and I get pneumonia?" Farmer Smith took a step back.

"I'll tell you what. Let's go look at the baptistry and I'll let you see it's not that deep and you can even feel how warm the water is," Pastor John reassured him. He looked at me. "Dove, do you mind turning on the lights in the baptistry?"

"Oh, sure." I started up the steps to the baptistry and reached for the light switch on the wall. I flipped the switch.

I gasped and then let out a scream.

Pastor John, along with the others, came running up behind me.

Floating in the water, cold and lifeless, was Eleanor Simmons.

*I* stopped stitching on my longarm machine to hear more clearly what the two women outside my room were saying.

"They suspect foul play," Agnes stated.

"Of course, they suspect foul play. Nobody drowns in a baptistry." Bertha snorted. "I bet Eleanor Simmons had never stepped foot into a baptistry until someone shoved her. That woman was pure evil. I can't believe she was actually related to poor Pastor John."

I poked my head out of the room. "Someone pushed her? Is that what killed her?"

Agnes cocked her head. "I was wondering when you would come out here and wait on us." She held up a swatch of fabric. "I need more of this Riley Blake fabric. I ran out before I could finish my quilt."

Taking the fabric from Agnes, I looked around the room. "We might have some over here." I walked over to the basket of remnant fabric and dug around until I found two fat quarters. "This is all that's left."

Agnes smiled. "That will be enough to finish my last block. I'm doing a Drunkards Path quilt for my neighbor."

"Speaking of a Drunkards Path, you realize Eleanor was fond of the drink?" Bertha cocked her head at me.

I sighed heavily. "So you've told me. Not that it's any of my business."

"How do you think she died, Dove?" Bertha narrowed her eyes on me like a hawk sizing up a mouse.

"How am I supposed to know? I'm no detective." Avoiding eye contact, I walked over to the register. I just wanted to do my job without getting involved in another case.

"The quilting club is worried that the police will try to pin this on Pastor John. Etta cracked under pressure when Dean questioned her. She spilled the beans about Pastor John and Eleanor getting in that argument and him threatening her." Agnes drew her lips into a thin line.

I snorted and shook my head. "I'm sure Dean will not try to pin the murder on anyone. He'll do his job as chief of police and investigate thoroughly. Besides, how do we know it wasn't just an accident?"

"Because a lot of people didn't like Eleanor. And the quilting club is meeting at your mom's house tonight to look at the facts in this case." Agnes's face broke into a wide grin. "Looks like we have a fresh case to solve. And we need you to lead it."

I held up my hands. "Hold on a minute. We should just leave this to the police and not get involved."

Bertha wedged in front of Agnes. "That's not what you said when Gertrude Brown was found dead in this shop."

"That's because I was a suspect. I was trying to clear my name since Dean seemed to drag his feet," I scowled. I wasn't sure I had forgiven my ex-boyfriend for not believing I was innocent from the start. Since moving back to Harland Creek after my disaster of a career in New York, I had a lot of baggage to figure out. That included my former high school sweetheart, Dean.

"It's not looking good for Pastor John. After the cops investigated the crime scene at the church, they went over to his home." Agnes gave me a knowing look. "I have it on good authority that some of the cops were seen removing items from his house."

"Since Sylvia lives across the street from the pastor, I'm assuming she's the one who told you this." I arched my brow.

"Maggie was there as well. Saw the whole thing," Bertha argued. "Look, I know you aren't really excited to be back here in Harland Creek, but this is your home, and Pastor John is family to all of us. We need to help get him out of this mess before he goes away for a crime he didn't commit. Besides, he put you on the prayer list when everyone thought you were the one who murdered Gertrude Brown."

I gasped. "He did?"

Agnes narrowed her eyes. "Remember how awful you felt when you were accused of murder?"

Guilt crawled around in my gut. "Well, what exactly do you expect me to do about it?"

"Go see Dean and see if he tells you if there are any other suspects. He'll tell you because he still has a thing for you." Bertha grinned.

I blinked. "No, he doesn't have a thing for me. He's dating Samantha Vaughn." I tried not to grimace as I said her name. Samantha was everything I wasn't. She had her own successful career as a pharmacist, owned her own business, and was a stunning brunette.

My career had taken a nosedive, I worked at my mom's quilt shop, and was a platinum blonde.

"I may not know a lot of things. But one thing I do know, and that's men. Dean Gray still has a thing for you. You're both too dang proud to admit it." Bertha clamped a hand on my shoulder. "Now get on over to the police station and charm your way into seeing the chief of police. You can tell us what you find out tonight when we all gather at your mom's." She turned on her heel. "Come on Agnes. I have things to do."

Agnes gave me a last nod as she and Bertha exited the shop.

I stood there waiting for the guilt of not doing anything to subside.

When it didn't, I grabbed my keys, turned the door sign to Closed, and headed over to the police station.

# CHAPTER 3

*I*t took less than five minutes before I was pulling up at the police station of Harland Creek. As soon as I killed the engine, my car backfired, and two cops leaning against their police car spun around.

I cringed and mouthed, 'I'm sorry' before crawling out of my car.

I hated to admit it, but my shallow side missed the expensive car I had in New York. I reminded myself that the hunk of junk I was driving was only temporary until I could get back on my feet again.

I grabbed my purse and slid out of the car. I glanced at my reflection in the driver's glass and tucked my T-shirt in my jeans before walking into the police station.

The front desk was empty, so I went straight to Dean's office.

The door was ajar, and I knocked once before I opened the door.

My mouth dropped.

Samantha Vaughn was perched on the corner of Dean's

desk while he sat in his chair, laughing at something she had said.

When his gaze met mine, the grin slid off his face.

"Dove."

"Sorry to interrupt. I can come back later." I turned to leave.

"No, wait. I was just about to leave." Samantha turned around and gave me a brilliant smile. "I was just dropping off some cookies for Dean. It was my first time baking this recipe that your mom gave me."

I hid my disdain for the woman and gave her a smile. "Oh yeah? Which recipe is that?"

"Tea Cakes. Your mom said Dean loves this recipe." Samantha blinked and looked back at Dean.

My mom had given Samantha her tea cake cookie recipe? What was she thinking? It was a closely guarded family recipe. I had to remember to have a talk with Mom when I got home.

"I'll give you two some privacy. Nice seeing you again, Dove." She gave me a little finger wave as she made her way out the door.

"This is certainly a surprise." Dean stood and studied me carefully.

"Yes, well. I just wanted to come by to see if you needed any more information from me about the...body." I swallowed and sat down in the chair opposite his desk.

He rested his arms on his desk and leaned forward. "No. I think we got all the information we needed from you yesterday. Everyone who was there when the body was discovered has already given their statements."

"Yeah. I heard about that. Etta seemed really chatty when telling everyone about the argument between Eleanor and Pastor John."

He narrowed his eyes at me. "How did you know that?"

I shrugged. "I overheard her telling Agnes in the fellowship hall."

"Overheard? Were you eavesdropping?" He cocked his head.

I grimaced. "No, I was just...out of sight."

A maddening grin played across his face. "You weren't trying to sneak a donut, were you?"

I stared at him and blinked. I hated he knew me so well.

"Back to the topic." I waved my hand in the air. "I just wanted to come down and let you know that I really don't think Pastor John had anything to do with this. I think this was an accident and not a murder."

"I won't officially know for sure until we get the report from the coroner's office." He looked at me.

"I mean, who would kill a woman in a baptistry? Certainly not Pastor John." I lifted my chin.

"Dove, why are you really here?"

I sighed and rolled my eyes. "Because I let Agnes talk me into seeing if you were going to pin the murder on the pastor."

He gave me a horrified look. "I would never pin a murder on anyone. I scrutinize every case that comes through this office. You act like we're a bunch of country bumpkins who run a corrupt police department."

I shook my head. "That's not what I meant."

"Right now, we are looking at Pastor John and his history with his sister. It seemed all was not as peaceful between them as he would like to have the town think."

"Dean, everyone has issues with their family. You don't seriously think he killed his sister?"

"I have business to do, and I'm sure your mom needs you back at the quilt shop."

His nonchalant attitude irritated me.

I gathered up my pride, and my purse, and stood.

He didn't even say goodbye as I walked out the door.

# CHAPTER 4

*T*hat night, after I had showered, I heard voices and headed downstairs to check it out.

"Pass me a macaroon, please, Weenie," Lorraine Chisolm said sweetly.

I stepped into the living room and spotted the entire group of Harland Creek Quilters sitting around a large whiteboard teetering against an artist's easel.

I crossed my arms and watched as the older ladies sipped tea and nibbled on sweets.

"Mildred, you must give me your tea cake cookie recipe. It's to die for." Elizabeth Harland sighed as she bit into one of Mom's cookies.

"Sounds like she's passing out the family recipe to anyone that asks." I shot my mom a look. It bothered me that she gave Samantha the recipe that Dean always loved.

"Dove!" My mom brightened when she noticed I was in the room. "So glad you decided to join us. We were just about to start our meeting."

"What meeting?" I snatched one of Elizabeth's sugar cookies off the plate and took a bite. They were my second favorite cookie in the world. My first was my mom's tea cake cookies.

"We are going to solve this case and get Pastor John off the hook for murder. Not that I would hold it against him even if he killed Eleanor," Bertha stated abruptly.

Elizabeth gaped at the woman.

My mom shot Bertha a stern look. "Bertha, Pastor John did not kill Eleanor. Don't even say such a thing."

"According to Etta, they were in a huge argument over her cutting off the funds for our missionaries."

"What an awful thing to do." Donna Williams shook her head.

"Eleanor was an awful person. Not sorry she's gone." Maggie Rowe scoffed.

The room grew silent.

Maggie frowned. "What?"

"Go ahead, Lorraine. Tell her." Elizabeth nodded.

"Tell me what?" Maggie glanced around the room.

Lorraine took a deep breath and blew it out. "There's a rumor in town that you had a confrontation with Eleanor the day before she died."

"Really?" Maggie snorted.

"It's more serious than that, Maggie," Agnes stated. "They have you on camera coming out of your building and meeting Eleanor in the alley. The video shows you slapping her."

Sylvia gasped. "Maggie, is that true? Did you slap Eleanor?"

Maggie lifted her chin. "So what if I slapped the old witch? Someone should have done it a long time ago." She set her coffee cup down, lifted her chin, and crossed her arms in defiance.

The silence in the room was unbearable, and I truly felt bad for Maggie. I had to do something.

"All right, let's not get all excited." I held out my hand. "Where's the dry-erase marker?"

"Here ya, go," Elizabeth handed it to me.

"Look, I'm a hundred percent sure that Maggie isn't the killer. And I know how it feels when someone accuses you of something you didn't do." I gave Maggie a sympathetic look. "So let's look at our list of possibilities and narrow them down one by one."

"Do we get to name them by quilt patterns again?" Weenie brightened. "I loved doing that. And I already have a name picked out for Pastor John."

I smiled at Weenie's enthusiasm. "What's the quilt name?"

"Cathedral Windows. Since he's a pastor." She smiled, looking pretty pleased with herself.

I blinked. "That's perfect, Weenie."

"Thank you." Her grin deepened.

I wrote Cathedral Windows on the whiteboard.

"Well, if I'm a suspect, then I get to pick my quilt block name." Maggie scowled.

"I don't think you can do that." Bertha shook her head.

"Then I'm going to leave." Maggie stood up.

"Let her pick her own quilt name or I'm leaving, too." Sylvia stood with her friend.

"I think it's only fair," I agreed. Everyone, except Bertha, nodded in agreement.

"What name do you want, Maggie?" Sylvia smiled at her friend.

"Wild Goose Chase. Because that's what you will find when you try to pin this murder on me. A wild goose case." She sat down and scowled.

I jotted it down while the rest of the room was trying to apologize to her.

"We are forgetting someone," I stated.

"Who?" Mom asked.

"The one person who is always at the church. In fact, I find it pretty odd that Etta told Agnes about the fight on the morning the victim was found dead," I said.

"Dove is right. Why, I just dropped off some pastries the day before to the pastor's office, and Etta didn't say anything about it." She narrowed her eyes at me. "Put her down, Dove."

"What do you want to call her?" I looked around the room.

"Bear Paw." Agnes nodded.

"Bear Paw? Why?" I asked.

"Because every time I see that woman, she is eating some kind of pastry. Usually it's a bear claw."

Made sense to me. I wrote it down. "Now what? We don't have any more suspects."

"I feel like we should go over to the pastor's house and investigate Eleanor's room. Bet she has a bunch of secrets in that room." Bertha stuffed a cookie in her mouth and chewed with a purpose.

"I'm sure the police got all the evidence they could find out of the house already," I stated.

"Maybe, but you never know what they might miss." Agnes agreed. "Besides, we should bring the pastor some food and get him distracted while someone goes upstairs to her room." Everyone turned and looked right at me.

"Me? No. I'm not going up to her room. That house gives me the creeps." I shook my head.

"I always found it weird that they still lived together after all these years." Weenie frowned.

"Well, one of the conditions of their father's will was that the family mansion stayed as it was and both Eleanor and Pastor John had to live there and it could never be sold. I heard Eleanor was the executor of the estate and practically made Pastor John beg for every dollar of his inheritance."

Sylvia frowned. "Now that she's gone, I guess Pastor John is the sole beneficiary."

The room grew uncomfortably quiet.

I cleared my throat. "I have a better idea of what we can do. Instead of going to the house, let's go back to the church and see if there are any clues that the police missed."

"Good thinking, Dove." Elizabeth brightened. "We should do it now, when no one is there. And I'll bring Petunia along."

Everyone stood.

"Wait, I don't think you can bring a goat into the church."

"Of course you can. She's the best detective we've got." Bertha nodded.

As the ladies filed out of the house, I couldn't help but feel like I had been upstaged by a goat.

*I* barely had time to dry my hair before driving over to the First Baptist Church. Mom rode with me while the other ladies followed behind.

"Park behind the church. I don't want to draw attention to ourselves by parking out front." Mom cast a worried glance at me.

"You know, we could just drive back home and forget all about this." I was tired and wanted to fall into bed.

She shook her head. "No. I can't do that. Pastor John needs help, and I don't want to let him down."

I pulled behind the church and parked. It was after ten o'clock and the rest of the sleepy town of Harland Creek was probably getting ready for bed. All the stores shut down around six and only a few houses we passed still had their lights on.

The rest of the ladies parked next to us behind the church. We were out of the car and walking up to the back door before Bertha could climb out of the van.

"Watch that goat, Elizabeth!" Bertha snarled. "The darn thing nearly ate a hole in my shoe."

"Petunia can't help it. She has a high metabolism," Elizabeth stated as she pulled on Petunia's leash to urge the goat to get out of the van.

Weenie stopped next to me and pressed her lips into a thin line. "Bertha knows better than to wear those stinky shoes. Petunia can't help it. Goats eat garbage."

I snorted.

"What was that? What are you two talking about?" Agnes narrowed her gaze on me.

I swear that woman has supernatural hearing.

"Weenie was just saying she forgot to put the garbage can out for the garbage truck tomorrow," I quickly covered.

Agnes shrugged. "Just do it before seven and you'll be alright." She looked at me. "Dove, go ahead and open the door."

"Me? Why me?"

"I don't want my fingerprints on the doorknob." Agnes stated.

I sucked my hand back into the sleeve of my shirt. Thank goodness it was getting cooler weather, and I had worn a long sleeve T-shirt. With my hand covered, I reached out and tried the knob. It turned.

"You guys should really think about locking up the church," I stated.

"What is someone going to steal? The hymnals?" Bertha gave me a snarl and shoved past me. She went straight to the fellowship hall, where I suspected she was going to check out the refrigerator.

"We got that new sound system." Weenie gave me a concerned look. "Someone could steal that."

"People won't steal from a church. They know better." Elizabeth walked in and headed straight for the baptistry.

I wished I had Elizabeth's confidence in people, but I had

seen too much of the world to know that all people were not inherently good.

"Let's go." Agnes nudged me in the direction where the crime had taken place.

I cringed. "I may need to check on Bertha. In the fellowship hall."

"No need, Dove." Sylvia stated. "She's already finished off the last of the donuts and is making herself a plate to take home from the leftovers in the kitchen."

"Fine." I forced my feet to walk in the direction of the baptistry.

When I got there, Elizabeth was already at the top of the stairs of the baptistry. She turned when we entered.

Petunia nudged me in the thigh and let out a bleat.

"They already drained the water out. Think we should step down inside and see if we find anything?" Elizabeth waited for an answer.

"I don't know. You're going to leave your DNA all over when you step inside." Maggie shook her head. "I say don't do it."

"What are you talking about?" Donna shook her head. "Her DNA is already all over the whole church. Every one of us goes here." Her gaze landed on me. "Well, almost everyone."

All eyes were glued on me.

"That's okay, Dove. I still pray for you." Weenie gave me a sweet smile.

"Thanks, Weenie. Good to know someone thinks I'm not bound for the alternative route for eternity." I walked up the steps and looked down to where Eleanor's body was found.

"I don't see anything here. I'm sure the police drained the water and went over everything with a fine-tooth comb."

"We need to be looking at how Eleanor got into the

21

baptistry. So whoever did it had to be strong enough to hold her under the water." I turned and looked at them.

"Are we even sure that's how she died? Drowning?" Sylvia asked.

"Officially?" Agnes shook her head. "No, but it's obvious. I mean, I got a good look at her and she had no marks on her."

"She's right. I talked to the coroner's assistant and he said they didn't see any marks on her when they brought her in." Lorraine nodded.

I frowned. "Okay, well since we are here, let's look throughout the sanctuary and see if anything looks out of place."

"Even the Sunday school rooms?" Weenie asked.

"Yes. Inspect every room thoroughly. And someone keep an eye on Petunia. We don't need her eating up half the church."

Petunia seemed to glare at me with her beady little eyes.

"I'll come with you, Dove." Maggie walked over to me. "Let's look in the sanctuary."

"Let's do it." We made our way through the door into the sanctuary and I flipped on the light.

The scent of Old English wood polish and old pew cushions hung in the air. The stained glass windows were dim in the dark but brought back childhood memories of how bright and pretty they were during the daylight.

Something caught the corner of my eye by the back door, and I froze.

"Who's there?"

Someone dressed in black popped up behind the pew and ran to the back door.

I sprinted to cut him off. "Stop!" I latched on around his waist but caught an elbow to the cheek.

I screamed in pain and crumpled to a heap on the floor.

"Dove!" Maggie hurried over and looked down at me. "Are you okay?"

I sat up and pulled my hand away from my face. There was blood on my hand.

I felt queasy and looked up at Maggie. "I don't feel so good."

The next thing I knew, the world grew dark.

# CHAPTER 6

"Ouch." I flinched as the paramedic, Ben Owens, put some medicine on my cheek. "That burns."

"Sorry." Ben held my cheek gently as he worked. "I don't want this to get infected, Dove."

"If it's just Bacitracin, I can put some medicine on it when I get home."

"What kind of paramedic would I be if I didn't give you a thorough physical assessment?" A grin played at the corners of his lips.

I felt my cheeks burn. I swallowed and reminded myself that Ben was just doing his job.

I looked up at him, surprised by how different he looked from when we went to high school together. Gone was the tall lanky nerd who poured over his books instead of going out with the other kids. His blue-eyed stare seemed to be scorching my cheek as he tended to my face. His uniform showed off his lean, muscular body and his biceps flexed every time he moved.

"Can I talk to her now?" Dean gave me a solemn look as he waited for Ben to finish assessing me.

"She doesn't need any stitches, but she hit her head when she fainted. She might need to come into the hospital to have her head looked at." Ben stepped back and looked at me.

"She didn't fall that far. She didn't pass out until she was already on the floor and saw the blood on her hand. I stuck my foot out to cushion her head." Maggie said helpfully.

"I'm not going to the hospital." I glared at him and his handsome face.

"That's not procedure, Dove." He cocked his head at me.

"I don't care. I'm not going." I crossed my arms over my chest and glared.

"Fine. But I'm going to have a talk with your mom about what symptoms of a head injury to look out for so she can watch over you and call the ambulance if needed." He gave me a pointed look and stepped back.

Dean narrowed his eyes at me. "What were you thinking coming into the church this late at night?"

"It's the house of God. I thought it was always open." I countered.

Ben snickered.

Dean shot him daggers as he put his stuff away.

I stood up from the pew and suddenly the room swam. I didn't want Ben to notice, so I eased back down on the pew. "You said you wanted to talk to me?" I looked up at Dean.

He shot Ben a look who finally took the hint and walked away, with Maggie trailing behind him asking questions about gout.

"Are you sure you're okay?" His gaze landed on my cheek.

"Yeah. Just an elbow to the cheek."

"Did you get a good look at who it was?"

"No. He was wearing black."

"Are you sure it was a male and not a female?" Dean cocked his head,

"Yeah. I'm sure. He was tall and skinny. But he wasn't

familiar. I don't think he was anyone that lives in Harland Creek." I rested my head against the pew and closed my eyes. "What about the autopsy? Was the cause of death drowning?"

"Dove, you know I can't tell you any details about this ongoing investigation." He rested a hip on the back of the pew.

"Dean. What are you doing to find the person who did this to Dove?" My mom hurried over and sat next to me and held my hand. "I can't believe there is so much crime going on in Harland Creek."

"Mom, there's hardly any crime."

"First Gertrude and now Eleanor." Bertha walked over. "It's going to be one of us next. Mark my words. Death comes in threes." She crossed her arms over her ample breasts.

"You think so?" Weenie gave me a worrying look. "Maybe I should get a gun, you know, for protection."

"Yeah. We should all get a gun." Agnes nodded vigorously.

"I already have a gun." Sylvia opened her handbag and pulled out a large revolver. She waved it around in the air.

Everyone ducked and Dean lunged for her hand. "Give me that." He took the gun away and unloaded it.

"Do you have a permit for this?" He scowled.

"I do. I got it after Eleanor kept coming by my shop, threatening me." Sylvia clamped her mouth shut when she realized what she had said.

Dean turned and gave her his full attention.

"Don't even give me that look, Dean. If she was shot to death then maybe I could be a suspect. But I'm not." She lifted her chin.

"I'm still going to need you to come down to the station and answer some questions for me." He propped his hands on his hips.

She scowled. "Can I come tomorrow after lunch? I have two perms in the morning."

"Fine." He huffed as she walked away with the rest of the quilting ladies and Petunia.

He turned back to me and shook his head.

"Dean, you know that Sylvia did not kill Eleanor." I forced myself to stand. The dizziness I felt earlier was gone.

"I know. But I want to know about Maggie. She doesn't have an alibi for the time of the murder. And she was on camera slapping Eleanor."

"She probably deserved a slap."

"Even if she did, she didn't deserve to be murdered." He reached out and gently touched my cheek. "We need to talk, Dove."

"Dean…"

His phone went off and he answered it. "Hey, Samantha."

My stomach dropped. I didn't want to stay there and listen to him talk to the woman he was currently dating.

He grabbed my arm, but I shrugged him off and shook my head.

I wanted to go home and go to bed and forget this night had ever happened.

## CHAPTER 7

*J* slept in the next morning and didn't arrive to the quilt shop until around eleven. My cheek was still sore from where I had been hit, and it had turned a delightful shade of purple, much to my chagrin.

I dressed comfortably that day, opting to wear jeans and my favorite pink sweatshirt since the temperature seemed to drop overnight.

I parked in front of Mom's quilt shop and hurried inside. A few customers were looking at fabric while Mom chatted with them. She gave me a smile when I entered, but I made a beeline for the backroom because I didn't want anyone to see me with a busted-up face.

Mom had already loaded a new quilt on the longarm machine for me to quilt. This was a Quilt of Valor made with patriotic colors of red, white, and blue. It was going to be a gift for a veteran in the nursing home.

I pulled out my phone and turned on Pandora. Stevie Nicks' "Dreams" came on after I clicked through some songs. I smiled and turned up the volume and sang along while setting up my next quilt.

I had been so busy getting the machine turned on that I jumped when I heard the voice. "Dove, do you have time to talk?"

I looked up at Pastor John's face.

"Sure. Come on in, Pastor John." I stepped back from my longarm machine and fumbled with my phone to turn off the music. I gave him a sheepish look. "Sorry about that."

He gave me a sad smile. "It's okay. Music helps pass the day." Pastor John had always been a thin man, but since Eleanor's death he looked like he'd lost ten pounds over the last few days. Dark circles hung under his worried eyes and his mouth was set in a worried frown.

All the years I had known Pastor John, I could never remember him frowning.

"How are you doing? I'm sorry I didn't get to speak to you at the church last night. The police were busy interrogating me to see if I saw who had hurt you."

"It's not your fault." I hesitated and then decided to come clean. I mean, if you couldn't tell a pastor the truth, who could you confide in?

"Pastor John, we were there looking for clues about Eleanor's...accident." I couldn't bring myself to use the word murder.

He pressed his lips into a thin line and nodded. "I figured as much when I saw the lights come on in the church."

"You saw us? Why didn't you come over?" It was my turn to frown.

He sighed heavily. "Because it's hard for me to even go inside the building since Eleanor's death. Last night when the police alerted me about the incident at church I walked over but stayed outside and answered their questions."

"Ah, that's why I didn't see you." I crossed my arms and rested a hip against the counter.

"It looks like that hurts." He nodded at my face.

29

"It looks worse than it is."

"You didn't get a good look at who did it?" He cocked his head.

"No. He was tall and wearing a black hooded sweatshirt, and after he elbowed me, I was focused on my pain and not him."

He let out a breath and shook his head. "I'm so sorry, Dove."

I nodded. "The quilters told me when I was a murder suspect that you prayed for me."

He gave a wry smile. "I knew you couldn't have killed Gertrude. The whole town knows how you react to the sight of blood."

I grinned. "Yes. Well. Not everyone thought I was innocent."

"I did. And a lot more people who knew your character realized you had nothing to do with it."

I cocked my head. "You know, Pastor John, Eleanor thought I did."

His eyebrows shot up, clearly shocked at this new piece of information. "I had no idea."

"So you weren't close with your sister? I mean, she didn't gossip about me to you?"

He gave a wry smile. "No, Dove. We might have lived in the same house but Eleanor never confided in me." He drew his brows together. "We've not been close since we were kids."

I couldn't imagine Eleanor as a child. "What was she like? As a kid, I mean." I wanted to know if she was always so cruel and mean to people.

"She was quite different from how she is now. I mean, how she was." He swallowed hard. "As a child, she was always following me around and wanting me to play board games with her. She was quite smart as a child, and could always beat me at games. I hate to admit it, but I hated playing with her. She was always following me around like a little puppy, and all I wanted to do was hang out with my friends." He ran his hand through his hair.

"Sounds like typical sibling drama to me."

"I know a lot of people didn't like Eleanor. But she wasn't always a cruel person." His brows knit together.

"What happened to make her change?" I asked.

His lips pressed into a thin line and I could tell by the set of his jaw, Pastor John did not appreciate my curiosity. "Some things are best left buried in the past, Dove." He gave me a pointed look. "It's best if you keep the quilting ladies out of this investigation."

A chill went up my spine. "Why is that?"

He shook his head and glanced at the door. "This has already hurt too many people. Just keep them out of this, okay?"

Just then, Agnes Jackson appeared at the door and smiled wide. "Hello, Pastor. I was just about to call you about…"

"I'm sorry, Agnes, I have to be going." He rushed out of the room and headed for the front door.

Agnes looked at me and scowled. "What in the world was that about?"

"You want me to be honest?"

"Of course."

"I think Pastor John knows more about Eleanor's death than he is letting on."

"Oh, Dove, he couldn't possibly…"

"All I know is he said for the quilting ladies to stop interfering. He said he didn't want to see anyone else hurt."

Agnes's eyes grew wide, and she went silent. That was a miracle. Agnes was never at a loss for words.

She looked at me and sighed. "I suppose you're going to tell us we can't investigate this crime."

I blinked and walked over to my phone. I turned on the music and then looked at her.

"I think you are all grown women. I have learned a long time ago that trying to wrangle you ladies is like trying to herd cats. Now, I'm going to go back to quilting."

"That's it?" Agnes scowled.

"No, I tend to get my best thinking when I'm sewing. Tell the other ladies to keep their ears open for any more information and we'll compare notes soon."

"So far, we have four suspects." I looked at Elizabeth, Agnes, and my mom across the kitchen table. Petunia was curled up on the kitchen rug taking a nap. They'd arrived early that morning to drop off some home-made eclairs, and we were sipping coffee and catching up.

"Four?" Elizabeth frowned and looked down at her note-book. "I have Pastor John as Cathedral Windows. Maggie as Wild Goose Chase and Etta as Bear Paw."

Agnes's eyes brightened. "We are forgetting the guy who elbowed Dove in the church."

I grinned. "Correct."

Elizabeth nodded. "Too bad we used Cathedral Windows on Pastor John. It would fit the fourth suspect perfectly since we found him in the church."

Mom nodded. "We need to name this guy." She looked over at me. "Dove, do you have any ideas?"

I sat back in my chair and took a bite of my eclair. As I contemplated, I chewed slowly. "I do. How about Jacob's Ladder?"

"Jacob was a righteous man in the Bible. The guy that hit you is far from righteous."

"Yeah. But Jacob also wrestled with the angel of the Lord. I can attest that my face felt like I'd been going a few rounds with this guy."

"I like it." Agnes nodded. She elbowed Elizabeth. "Write Jacob's Ladder."

Elizabeth jotted the name down on the paper. "Maybe this case will get solved quick." She looked up. "It gives me the creeps to think there's someone among us who could be a killer."

"Don't worry. This will be over soon and everyone can get back to business as usual." I smiled.

"Speaking of business as usual. I need you to run to the grocery store and pick up some things, Dove." Mom wiped her hands with a napkin. "The quilting ladies are each taking turns and making a meal for Pastor John. And I guess we need to be planning on making a meal after the funeral service, so I'll need some things for that." She stood. "I'll make a list." She headed into the living room to grab the notepad she kept in her purse.

"I haven't heard when the funeral will take place. Have you?" Elizabeth looked at Agnes.

"No. But they can't have it until the coroner has released the body," Agnes stated. "I'm sure we'll know more information soon."

Mom returned with her pen and pad in hand. She finished scribbling something on the paper and ripped it from the pad. "Here ya go, Dove. Leave nothing off. I plan on making enough for Pastor John to for a few days."

Sighing, I stood and took the paper. "I'll get right on this." I headed upstairs to get ready.

Thirty minutes later, I was walking through the doors of the grocery store with the list in my hand.

"Hello, Dove!" Colin Bennet greeted me in the produce aisle. He was the English owner of the bookstore in Harland Creek. He'd moved to town a couple of years ago and we had met when I bought the latest Jodi Thomas novel in his bookstore, The English Rose.

"Hi, Colin." I smiled and glanced in his basket at the four steaks and large potatoes he was carrying. "Looks like you and Gabriela are going to have some leftovers."

"Oh, we are having another couple over for dinner tonight. Dean and Samantha."

My smile slid off my face. "I see."

He frowned. "Is anything wrong?"

"Oh no. I … I just didn't realize Samantha liked steak." I quickly lied.

Colin blinked. "You know, I just assumed she did. I mean, I see her at the diner all the time and it's certainly not the healthiest place to eat."

"You are probably right. I'm sure she'll love the ribeye." I forced a smile.

His girlfriend, Gabriela, walked up with a head of lettuce in her hand. "They are out of fresh tomatoes, so I figured we'd just grab a couple at Aunt Agnes's house." She looked at me and smiled. "Hey Dove. Glad to see you're not the prime suspect of a murder investigation this time around."

"Me too." I admitted.

His eyes knit together in a frown. "Maybe I should go see if they have any filets. Not everyone likes ribeye." He cast a look at Gabriela. "I'll be right back."

Gabriela looked at me. "What's that about?"

I shrugged. "I don't know. I think he was wondering if Samantha was a picky eater."

Gabriela grinned "Ah Dean and Samantha. How do you feel about them dating? Does it bother you?"

"No." I frowned. "I don't care who Dean dates." I straightened my shoulders.

"Right." Gabriela snorted. "Look, just between me and you, I don't think he's over you."

I blinked and then shook my head. "Of course he is. It's been years since we dated in high school."

"Yeah well…"

The sound of raised voices had us both looking around.

Pastor John came fast walking down aisle two with a box of macaroni and cheese under his arm. Suddenly, Lester Hammond came down the aisle after him.

Lester Hammond was a retired veteran who lived in one of the trailers in the RV park Eleanor had owned. She'd bought it after Gertrude Brown was killed. She'd promised to renovate the Chateau RV park into something beautiful, but after a few complaints from the longtime residents, she'd gone back on her promise and raised the rent.

He shook his fist in Pastor John's face. "You have that money now. Of course, you need to do the renovations. The leak in my roof has gotten bigger and with the winter coming, I need it fixed."

"I know, but I don't have the money. We have to wait until the investigation is closed, and the life insurance is paid out."

"Insurance?" Lester frowned. "I'm talking about the huge inheritance your daddy left you and Eleanor. The whole town knows Eleanor was left in charge of the money. With her gone, you need to do the Christian thing and fix the RV park."

"Lester, I can't do that. You're just going to have to wait until they settle the case."

Lester narrowed his eyes and poked his finger in Pastor John's chest. "I'm getting fed up, waiting on the likes of people like you and your sister. You're no better. You may carry a Bible, but you don't have me fooled. You don't have anyone fooled. You better watch yourself or you'll end up floating in a baptistry yourself." He glared before storming out of the store.

I rushed over to Pastor John with Gabriela on my heels.

He looked at me with fear in his eyes.

"Are you okay, Pastor?" I touched his shoulder.

He flinched at my touch and put the box of mac and cheese on the nearby shelf. "I have to go."

He hurried out of the store.

"I've never seen him like that." Gabriela said softly.

"I know." I hurried over to the window and saw Lester peel out of the parking lot in an old blue and white Ford truck.

There was no mistake that Lester Hammond had threatened the pastor. It seemed like the two had more history than what I thought.

I made a mental list to add Lester Hammond to our list of suspects before grabbing a buggy to shop.

# CHAPTER 9

"*T*hat's a lot of food." I scanned the food in various casserole dishes that lined the kitchen counter.

"This is the South, Dove." Mom nodded her head. "You always feed the grieving family. It's just how we Southerners communicate our sympathy."

I peeled back the Saran wrap from a platter and snatched a sugar cookie. Mom swatted my hand but she was too late. I already shoved it in my mouth. Mom only shook her head.

"All of this is for Pastor John?" I took a sip of my water.

"Yes."

I sighed. "And I suppose I'm going to be the one taking all this over to his house."

"You'll have company." Mom grinned.

"I will? Who?"

"I'm coming of course, and Elizabeth will be going over there with us as well as…"

I held up my hand. "Let me guess. Agnes is coming. Those two are thick as thieves."

Mom gave a nervous laugh. "Not exactly. Someone closer than Agnes?"

I frowned.

She looked at me. "Petunia."

My mouth dropped. "The goat? We can't take a goat to the pastor's house."

"Yes we can. Elizabeth said Petunia would be a distraction and it would give you time to explore Eleanor's room for clues." Mom brightened.

It began to scare me how the quilters thought this was one big puzzle to solve and not some serious crime.

"How do you know Pastor John is even going to let us in the door with a goat?"

Mom blinked. "I don't. But I guess I just have to have faith." She picked up a casserole dish. "Now help me load the car. Elizabeth should be here any minute."

Less than ten minutes later, I was driving Mom, Elizabeth, and Petunia over to the pastor's house.

"Stop chewing on my hair." I swatted at Petunia's head.

"She loves you. She's just giving you kisses, Dove." Elizabeth chuckled.

I wiped my hand through the back of my hair where she'd tried to eat my hair. "Tell her I prefer flowers from people I love."

"I already updated the quilters about what you witnessed in the grocery store with Lester. So we need to add him to the list of suspects." Mom looked over her shoulder at Elizabeth. "Didn't Bertha say he moved to Mississippi from Arkansas?"

"Sure did." Elizabeth nodded.

"Then we should name him Arkansas Traveler."

"Great idea. I did an Arkansas Traveler quilt for my niece when she went to college. Turned out nicely." Elizabeth added.

I pulled up to the pastor's house, parked and quickly got out. I had already popped the trunk and was picking up a casserole dish when Elizabeth came around the back of the car.

"Now, the first chance you get, go upstairs to Eleanor's room and see if you can find anything that might tell us who the killer is." Elizabeth grabbed a plastic container with cookies and tugged on Petunia's leash toward the front door.

"I doubt it's going to be that easy," I sighed.

"And be sure to check the panty drawer," Mom added and picked up a sweet potato casserole.

I shook my head and walked up to the front door. I looked up at the three story, yellow brick Victorian inspired mansion. Two evergreens sat in concrete planters on either side of the door.

It was the largest house in Harland Creek and had been in the family forever. It was known that the Simmons family got their money from the great-grandfather's oil business. All the men in the family had gone into law, all except Pastor John.

Elizabeth rang the doorbell and I was surprised by the melodious sound.

The door swung open and Pastor John blinked when he saw us. "Ladies? I wasn't expecting company."

Mom patted his arm and moved past him into the house. "That's because we didn't call. We brought you food. I know it's hard being alone at a time like this with no one to cook for you."

Elizabeth walked in behind her and snorted. "I highly doubt Eleanor ever cooked."

Mom shot her a look.

Pastor John looked at me and I held up my casserole dish. "Which way is the kitchen?"

"At the end of the hallway." He gave me a forced smile and stepped out of the way to let me into the house.

I led the way to the kitchen with the ladies, and Petunia followed behind me.

When I stepped into the kitchen I stopped. It was stunning. Despite it being an older house, the kitchen had recently been updated with fresh white quartz countertops and painted cabinetry with new handles and pulls. There was new open-air lighting over the island counter with new plush kitchen stools.

"This is gorgeous." I looked to the pastor.

"Yes, well, Eleanor had it updated very recently." He nodded.

"Did she design it herself?" I set the dish down and looked around the room.

"Oh no. She used an interior designer." He glanced at Petunia. "Would she be more comfortable outside, in the backyard maybe?"

"Oh no. She's housebroken." Elizabeth stroked the goat's head.

"I see." Pastor John looked uncomfortable.

"I'll get the rest of the food."

"There's more?" His eyebrows shot up.

"We made a lot of food so you don't have to worry about dinners for the next few days." Mom patted his arm. "Now let's go into the living room while Dove finishes getting the food out of the car."

"Why don't we go into my study." He corralled the ladies and goat out of the kitchen.

I made quick use of my time getting the rest of the food inside and putting it away in the large refrigerator.

The pastor's study was near the front of the house so I knew I had only a few minutes to get upstairs and have a look around before he came looking for me.

I crept up the curving staircase to the second floor. The floor creaked. I froze and held my breath but when I realized

41

Pastor John hadn't heard, I continued on my trek. On the second floor there were a lot of doors to choose from so I tried each door and peaked in. One was a bathroom, another was a sitting room, and another was a guest bedroom. I opened the next door and looked inside. This room was different from the others. This was a woman's bedroom. I looked at the portrait hanging over the fireplace and shivered. Eleanor Simmons, dressed in black, was staring back at me in the painting.

I sucked up my courage and stepped inside the room.

I had the weirdest feeling that Eleanor was looking at me from her painting. I turned my back away from her and looked around the room.

The bed was an expensive canopy bed with bedding in dark maroon. The wallpaper was cream and black toile pattern. There was a secretary desk along the wall and a single nightstand with a Tiffany-style lamp. A single chest of drawers sat near the window. Other than the portrait there was nothing personal in the room.

I opened the nightstand drawer and pulled out a book of poems. I snorted. Definitely wouldn't have figured Eleanor for a lover of poems.

Walking over to the chest, I opened the top drawer. Inside were some silk nightgowns and some pantyhose.

I grimaced and opened the second drawer. It was her panty drawer. I held my breath and rifled through the undergarments, praying I wouldn't find anything. There was something creepy about searching through a dead women's panties.

My fingers brushed against something cold. I pulled it out and held it up.

It was a gold necklace with the letter M.

My stomach dropped.

There was only one woman in Harland Creek with this same exact necklace.

And that person was Maggie Rowe.

I thought I heard a thud. I stilled and looked around the room. I didn't see anything, but my fear was palpable. My heart pounded in my chest.

I heard footsteps in the hallway and I quickly stuffed the necklace in my jeans pocket. I looked around the room, contemplating a place to hide but couldn't find one.

I was suddenly frozen in fear as the door opened.

## CHAPTER 10

"*P*etunia?" I went over to the goat and grabbed her leash. "You are in so much trouble."

"What's going on in here?" Pastor John appeared in the doorway. He frowned when he spotted me. "Dove? What are you doing in Eleanor's room?"

"Sorry. I was trying to capture Petunia. I found her in here." I looked at the goat and glared. "Bad goat, Petunia. No snacks for you tonight."

She let out a bleat.

"How did Petunia get in?" He cocked his head. "The door was locked."

I shrugged. "Don't ask me. That goat has been known to find a way into rooms before. She's pretty smart for a goat," I chuckled.

"Petunia?" Elizabeth called from downstairs.

"Come on." I tugged on Petunia's leash and led her out of the room into the hallway. I walked her over to the landing and looked down. "Elizabeth, Petunia is up here."

"Upstairs? Why that little rascal. I turned my head for one second and next thing I knew she was gone. We checked the kitchen because I know how much she loves cookies." Elizabeth said loudly.

Pastor John appeared at my arm. "We're coming down."

I started down the stairs but the pastor grabbed my arm. "Dove. I know you are trying to help. But please. Don't." He tightened his grip.

"I don't know what you mean." I tried to tug out of his grasp but he was pretty strong.

"This is none of your business. Just let things go. Eleanor is gone now and there's nothing anyone can do to bring her back. Just let it go and stop snooping. Get busy making a life for yourself."

I lifted my chin. "I'm not snooping. I'm trying to get Petunia downstairs. I do have a life you know." His words stung. Even if they were true.

He gave me one last determined look before he let me go.

I tightened my hold on Petunia and walked the goat downstairs. She got sidetracked a couple of times by the floral wallpaper but I herded her downstairs.

"There's my girl." Elizabeth clapped her hands together and bent to hug Petunia. I looked at Mom expecting some love myself, but she was too busy keeping her eyes on Pastor John who was still upstairs.

"I'm sorry ladies. You will have to see yourselves out. I have some business upstairs that I need to see to." He gave a polite smile and turned to walk down the hallway.

Mom and Elizabeth exchanged glances and then looked at me.

"Let's go." I headed for the door with the ladies and Petunia on my heels.

Once outside they walked on either side of me.

"In all my years, Pastor John has never let me leave his house without walking me to my car." Elizabeth cocked her head.

"Me too. That was way out of character for him." Mom shook her head. "Dove, did you find something upstairs?"

"Get in the car first." I unlocked the door and held the doors open for them.

"You did. I knew you would find something." Elizabeth gave me a grin. She let Petunia get in the backseat before she slid in next to the goat. Mom climbed into the passenger's seat.

I hurried around and got into the driver's seat and started the car.

"Well, what did you find?" Mom asked.

"You're not going to be happy."

"Dove, stop stalling and tell us." Elizabeth stated firmly.

"Fine." I stuck my hand in my jeans pocket and pulled out a necklace. "I found a necklace. A necklace that belongs to Maggie."

## CHAPTER 11

"*I*'m going over to talk to Maggie." I looked at Mom across the breakfast table.

"You sure that Elizabeth hasn't already called and told her what we found in Eleanor's room?" Mom gave me a worried look.

"No. Elizabeth promised me that she would say nothing until I told Maggie we found her necklace. Besides, I want to get Maggie's honest reaction when I show her the necklace."

"Dove," Mom touched my arm. "You don't really think Maggie had anything to do with Eleanor's death do you?"

"I'm pretty sure she's innocent."

"Pretty sure, isn't completely sure." Mom's eyebrows knit together. "I've known Maggie all my life. We went to school together. I'm sure she couldn't have killed Eleanor."

"I thought the same about Patricia, but she ended up being the one who murdered Gertrude." I crossed my arms and sat back in the chair.

"That's true." Mom sighed heavily. "I guess I need to get ready to head into the shop. I have a Grandmother's Flower

47

Garden quilt that I need to finish up. Bye, honey." She grabbed her purse and headed out the door.

I needed to get going as well. I gathered my purse and slipped my shoes on before heading out to my car.

I drove slowly and looked at all the homes along the street. When I was a kid, Harland Creek seemed so big but now, it seemed small. Maybe that's why I left in the first place. To find my place in the world.

Look how that turned out.

Back at home, with a failed career and no plan or direction on where I was in life.

The more I thought about it, the more depressed I began to feel.

I turned into the parking lot of the new donut shop and hurried inside to seek the one thing I knew would boost my spirits.

The bell tinkled overhead as I walked inside.

A familiar figure dressed in overalls was paying for an order of a dozen glazed donuts. He turned and gave me a look of surprise.

"Hey, Dove." Farmer Joe Smith lifted his cowboy hat in a greeting.

"Hey, Farmer Joe. I just stopped in to get some donuts. Thought it would brighten my day." I sighed heavily and let my gaze wander over the glass display.

He snorted. "Ever since the "incident", he cleared his throat, "I've come in here every morning for their coffee and glazed donuts." He shook his head. "I don't sleep well at night so I need all the caffeine I can get."

I frowned at him. "Are you okay, Farmer Joe?"

He looked around the room nervously and then set his gaze on me. He leaned in and lowered his voice. "That could have been me in that baptistry. I could have drowned. What if I had shown up at the church early and the killer drowned me instead?"

My heart tugged for the older man. "Oh, Farmer Joe. I don't think that's true. I mean, we still don't know the actual cause of death. Maybe she tripped, fell in, and hit her head. It's too soon to know anything definite."

He leaned back, licked his lips and cast one last nervous glance around the donut shop. "You never know Dove. People are dropping like flies around here. Just keep your eyes peeled and be alert." He hurried out the door.

I wasn't sure what to think.

After I got my order, I took one donut out of the bag and began eating. I decided to walk over to Maggie and Sylvia's shop instead of driving since it was just down the block.

The weather was nice. Trees were changing colors and the sky was a brilliant robin's-egg blue. I always loved fall. It reminded me of pumpkins and bonfires and warm fuzzy blankets.

Dean first asked me out in junior high during a football game. It was cool enough that people were wrapped up in blankets in the stands.

This time of year always reminded me of Dean. When the first colored leaf fell in New York it reminded me of him.

Shaking my head, I finished off my second donut and stuck the bag in a garbage bin.

I smiled at the S&M salon that Sylvia and Maggie had unwittingly named.

I opened the door and stepped inside. The scent of perm solution was almost overwhelming.

Sylvia was busy putting rollers in Mrs. Wither's hair while a line of ladies was up under dryers, reading magazines. Maggie was putting the final touches on Mrs. Hollingworth's blowout and laughing at something the old woman said.

"Why, Dove! Did you come in to get your hair done?" Sylvia smiled and walked over to me.

"Not today, Sylvia. I just dropped by to talk to Maggie." I looked around the room. "Looks busier than I have ever seen it."

Sylvia arched a brow and leaned in closer. "We have a lot more customers now that Eleanor is gone."

I frowned. "How's that?"

"Eleanor threatened some of the women that if they came in here to get their hair done, she wouldn't support their charities." Sylvia glanced over her shoulder at the woman sitting in Maggie's chair. "Mrs. Hollingsworth depended on Eleanor's monthly donation to help with her husband's expenses for his cancer treatment. She told Mrs. Hollingsworth if she ever got her hair done here, she would stop helping with her husband's expenses."

My eyes widened. "That's awful. Why would Eleanor do that?"

"Because that's how she controlled people. She threatened them financially." Sylvia looked over her shoulder. "Maggie is finished if you want to talk to her."

"Thanks, Sylvia." I touched her shoulder before walking over to the stylist station.

Maggie brightened. "Dove. What a nice surprise. If you want a hair appointment, you'll have to come back tomorrow. We are covered up in customers today."

"I'm not here for an appointment, I'm here to talk. Is there somewhere we can go that's more private?"

"Let's go to the back. I just put on a new pot of coffee." Maggie led the way and I followed.

I looked around the small but cozy space Sylvia and Maggie had created as a break room.

There was a small pub-style table with two chairs in the corner. The small kitchenette had a sink and a couple of overhead cabinets. Maggie pulled down two pink mugs and poured us two cups of coffee. She handed me one and set the cream and sugar on the pub-table for me to doctor my coffee.

"Thanks." I added cream and sugar and then sat down. Maggie sat across from me on the other side.

Maggie took a sip of her black coffee "What's up, Dove? Do you have some information on the case? Your mom mentioned something about Lester and the pastor getting into an argument in the grocery store. She said you saw everything."

"Yeah. It was pretty disturbing. Lester seems to think he's owed repairs on his trailer and since Eleanor is dead, Pastor John should make good on that promise."

"I don't blame, Lester." Maggie's eyes narrowed as she sipped her coffee. "Eleanor made a lot of threats to a lot of people. I think Eleanor got what was coming to her."

My gut tightened at her words. I had known Maggie all my life. When I was a child, Maggie had been my first Sunday school teacher. In middle school Maggie had given me my first and only perm. And when I graduated high school, Maggie had given me a silver charm bracelet.

"Maggie, did you have any reason to be upset with Eleanor?"

She snorted. "Of course I did. She kept wanting to buy our building. I had already told her no."

"Is that why you slapped her?" I was referring to the slap caught on video.

Maggie straightened and set her coffee down. "Now listen here, Dove. I don't know what you are getting at, but I didn't kill Eleanor. Besides, if I was going to do her in, I would have used my hands." She held up her perfectly mani-cured fingers.

"I'm going to be really honest." I set my coffee down. "I

don't think you killed Eleanor. I've known you all my life. I need to tell you something. I went into Eleanor's room."

Maggie's eyes widened and she leaned forward. "Did you find something?"

"I did." I pulled the necklace out of my jean's pocket and held it up. "Is this yours?"

She blinked before she reached out for it. "Where did you find it?" She turned the necklace over in her hands.

"In Eleanor's room."

Her eyes widened. "That little witch. She stole it."

"Why would she steal it? I mean, Eleanor was a rich woman."

Maggie's eyes narrowed on me. "She stole it because it meant something to me. That's how Eleanor was. She'd take anything from anyone if it meant something to them. She was mean for sport." She stood and stuck the necklace in her pocket. "Now if you will excuse me, I have another customer."

"But Maggie…"

She held up her hand, effectively cutting me off. "I'm not going to talk about Eleanor Simmons any more today. I've had my fill." She headed out of the breakroom leaving me alone.

I put my coffee in the sink and decided to leave through the back door.

I couldn't help but think Maggie was hiding something, something that had to do with Eleanor's death.

## CHAPTER 12

o take my mind off worrying over Maggie and if she was somehow involved in the murder of Eleanor, I pulled out my sketchbook during my lunch break and began drawing out a new design for a pantsuit. I'd gotten an email a few days ago from a manufacturer who was interested in some of my fashion drawings. It had made me think it was a sign to start getting back into what I really loved doing, just maybe doing it in a different way.

I emailed them back and they gave me a deadline for some designs.

I'd always designed children's clothing when I was in New York. I liked the smaller scale and how I could be more imaginative with the fabrics and styles. But after I successfully made myself a dress, I decided to try a pantsuit.

I sipped my coffee and once I had my design sketched out, I picked up my colored pencils and began coloring the fabric.

"Wow, that's really pretty." Mom looked over my shoulder.

"Thanks. I'd like to try to make this but we don't have the

right fabrics in the shop. I might have to drive over to Jackson this weekend and find something." I cocked my head and colored in the lapel of the jacket.

"Or you could go over to Stacey's and check out her stock of fabric."

I sat upright. "Stacey Landers? The owner of Bettie's Boutique? I thought she got her clothes shipped in? I didn't know she had fabric."

"The company she gets her clothes from accidently crossed their wires. Instead of a shipment of clothes, she got a shipment of fabric. She asked if I wanted to come buy it from her, but I haven't had time to run over there."

"I'd love to have a look." I glanced at the time on the microwave.

"Go ahead and go now. We're pretty slow and the quilt you're working on can wait." Mom patted me on the shoulder.

"You sure?"

"Absolutely. Enjoy yourself and don't rush back."

I put my coffee cup in the sink and ran to the sewing room and grabbed my purse. As I walked out to get in my car, my mind raced with different design ideas.

By the time I pulled up to Bettie's Boutique, I had five different designs for holiday dresses.

I stepped inside the cute boutique and looked around for Stacey.

She was in the back and looked up from helping a customer pick out shoes when I walked in.

"Hey, Dove! I'll be with you in a second."

"No rush." I smiled and looked around the store. Stacey had some cute items but nothing like I had been dreaming up.

"Hey, Dove. What can I do for you? We just got a shipment of fall sweaters that are super cute."

"I'll have to take a look. But that's not why I'm here." I leaned in. "My mom said you got a shipment of fabric in by mistake. I was wondering if I could take a look."

"Please, be my guest." She started walking toward the back and I followed. "I can't believe I got fabric instead of my new blouses. It's going to cost me a fortune in shipping to send it back so that's why I asked your mom if she was interested." She opened the door to the stockroom.

Inside there were rolling hangers filled with clothes not yet tagged for sale. To the side were open boxes of bolts of fabric.

"This is a lot of boxes." I bent to look inside the first box. There were at least four bolts of different types of fabric. Some were more suited for evening dresses while others were best suited for casual wear.

A customer called out from the store. Stacey sighed. "Take your time Dove. Pick out as much as you like, I'm only asking ten dollars per bolt."

"Ten dollars? That's all?" I gaped.

"Since it's the manufacturer's fault they are shipping my clothes next week at no cost to me." She looked toward the store. "I do have one more person coming to look, so make sure you get what you want before she gets here. It's an interior designer. I'll leave you to look." She smiled and headed back into the store.

I couldn't believe my luck. I eased to my knees. I pulled my sketch pad out of my purse and set it on the floor beside the boxes. I began pulling out bolts of fabric and holding it next to my sketchbook. I piled up the bolts I wanted next to the wall as I went from box to box.

"Oh, I didn't realize anyone was back here." An older woman with short blonde hair and large glasses appeared at the door. She was in her late fifties, petite, and accentuated her Prada pantsuit and purse with stacks of gold jewelry on her wrist and neck. "Stacey told me to come back and look at the fabric."

I stood. "Oh yes. You must be the interior decorator. Hi, I'm Dove Agnew." I held out my hand.

"Hi, I'm Victoria Felts." She took my hand. "Have you gotten all the good fabrics?" She arched her eyebrow.

It made me laugh. "I have a pile over there." I pointed. "There's still a lot to go through."

She nodded. "I have a client who needs some pillows to match their bedroom chairs."

"Oh yeah? What color are you looking for?"

"Something light blue or silver." She opened the box I'd already gone through and pulled out a bolt of blue sateen. She frowned and stuck it back.

"There is a pretty silver fabric in the bottom of this box." I opened the top. "The fabric was too heavy for what I'm looking for, but you might like it." I pulled out the bolt.

Her eyes lit up. "Oh, that is nice." She took it from me and rubbed the fabric between her fingers.

"Are you new in Harland Creek? The only interior designer I know that lives here is Allison Jackson." I opened the next box.

Victoria looked up and blinked. "I don't know her. I don't live here. I live in Jackson. I was first contacted to do a job here a few months ago for a kitchen remodel. After that, I've picked up a few clients here."

I stopped digging through the fabric. "Kitchen remodel? It wouldn't happen to be the Simmons' house would it?"

She looked at me and rolled her eyes "Yes. It was."

"I saw the kitchen the other day, and it's fabulous. You did a really great job." I added.

"Thank you. But the owner didn't think so." She pressed her mouth into a frown.

"You're kidding me."

"I don't kid." She blinked and looked at me.

A shiver ran up my spine at the vibe she was giving off.

"Eleanor thought I did such a bad job that she refused to pay. So I slapped her arrogant butt with a lawsuit. She told me I would never win because she knows the judge personally." Victoria's mouth curled into a grin. "Eleanor Simmons had no idea who she was dealing with. I informed her that I always get my money. One way or the other."

I swallowed hard. "I see. But now that she's dead isn't that going to be hard to get your money?"

Victoria laughed and clutched the bolt of fabric to her chest. "Darling. It's easier to get money from a dead horse than you realize. All I'm waiting on is for the estate to settle and Pastor John to send me a check." She blinked and cocked her head. "It's funny. People just don't realize how much time they have left on this earth. They think time is limitless." She laughed and gathered her bolt. "I have to be going."

I watched Victoria Felts sashay out of the room with the bolt of blue I had recommended.

I didn't know the woman but questions rose up in my mind.

I realized then that our suspect list just got longer.

## CHAPTER 13

he next morning was Saturday and my day off. But after a sleepless night, I got up around six and padded downstairs in the T-shirt I'd slept in. It was one of Mom's and had a giraffe on it with the words 'Good Morning' splayed across the bottom. As an adult I knew I needed proper sleepwear but I was still watching my pennies.

After the coffeepot started brewing I crept out onto the back porch with a blanket and sat in a patio chair to wait.

It was just getting light and the neighborhood was still asleep. I curled up in my chair and thought about how everything was changing. Maggie was mad at me for thinking she was a murder suspect. I still hadn't figure out what I was going to do for a career, and Dean had moved on to Samantha Vaughn.

All these things made my stomach hurt.

The idea of moving to a town five states away where no one knew me was very appealing. Now if I only had the funds to do something about it.

"Dove?"

I let out a scream and jumped out of the chair at the sound of my name.

I pressed my hand to my chest where my heart was threatening to beat out of my chest.

"What are you doing? Trying to scare me to death?"

"Sorry. I knocked on the front door, but when I saw the light on back here I just walked around." His gaze drifted down to my bare legs and then back to my T-shirt.

I shifted my weight and my face heated. I was practically half naked and standing in front of my ex-boyfriend.

"What are you doing here?" I asked with annoyance in my voice.

"I have some questions." He crossed his arms over his chest.

"It's too early for questions; I haven't had my coffee yet."

He waved his hand to the door. "Then let's get you some coffee."

I headed inside to the kitchen and Dean followed.

I headed to the laundry room and found some denim shorts and pulled them on before coming back to the kitchen.

A smile played on Dean's lips. "Don't get dressed for me. I was enjoying the view."

I shot him a scowl. "You better not let Samantha Vaughn hear you say something like that." I pulled down a mug from the cabinet and looked at him. "Want a cup?"

"Sure."

I pulled another coffee mug down and began pouring two cups of coffee. "So what are you doing here?"

He took his coffee and held open the back door. I followed him out and we both sat. I pulled the quilt over my bare legs and sipped my coffee.

"I'm here because I want to know if you found out anything about this case."

"Why are you asking me for help? You're the chief of police. I'm just a law-abiding citizen."

"Because I spotted Agnes Jackson following Etta around the square with binoculars. Every time Etta stopped to talk to someone, Agnes would duck behind a tree or a bush. Tell your quilting ladies they need to stop acting like Columbo."

I barked out a laugh. "If you think I can control what the quilting ladies do, you give me far too much credit. You said Agnes was following Etta around?"

He nodded.

"That's actually smart. I almost forgot about Etta being a suspect. I mean she was the one who told Agnes about an argument between Eleanor and Pastor John. I'm kind of surprised she even told you about it. I always thought Etta would do anything to protect Pastor John."

"Protect him? Why would she need to protect him?" He cocked his head.

I shook my head. "You mistook my meaning. I mean, Etta almost acts like she's in love with Pastor John. She's an old maid who never married. She's always been protective of him. If she really thought he committed murder then she wouldn't be telling the police anything negative about Pastor John."

"Is that so? How do you figure?" He stretched out his long legs and sipped his coffee.

"Because when you're in love with someone you protect them. At all costs." I huffed. Sometimes Dean was pretty dense when it came to emotional stuff.

"Can I ask how the case is going? Or is that off-limits?" I eyed him.

"I'm sure it will be all over town by the time the sun sets today but… I have the official cause of death."

I sat up in my chair.

"Drowning. And she had a blow to the back of the head as

well. It was small and that's why it wasn't noticed right away."

"So it really was murder."

"Were you expecting a different outcome?" He looked at me strangely.

I shrugged. "I don't know. I feel like I don't understand people sometimes."

"Me and you both." He stared at me and I felt like his words were aimed at me.

"Speaking of suspects, have you looked at Lester Hammond?"

"The veteran who lives at the RV Park?"

"Yes. I heard him yelling at Pastor John in the grocery store. He said that now that Eleanor was out of the way, there was no reason not to make good on the promise of fixing up the trailers."

Dean leaned forward on his knees. "I've known Lester since I was a little kid. I don't think he'd kill Eleanor."

"I didn't think Patricia was capable of murder and look what happened."

He sighed heavily and stood. "Any more suspects you want me to investigate?" He smirked.

"Yes. Look into Victoria Felts. She was the interior designer for Eleanor. She redid the kitchen and Eleanor didn't pay her. Victoria said she always gets paid. No matter what."

Dean rolled his eyes. "Really Dove? An interior designer? You'd do better to suggest the guy who elbowed you in the church as a suspect."

"Yeah, what about him?" I jumped up out of my chair. The quilt dropped to the floor and the chill of the morning made me wrap my hands around my chest.

"No trace of him. We think he was a runaway teen

passing through. He was probably sleeping in the church until you ladies came in and scared him half to death."

I narrowed my eyes at him. "Well that poor runaway teen drew blood." I pointed to my cheek. The bruise and swelling had gone away but I still had a mark on my face.

"I need to be going." He set his cup on the patio table.

I bit my lip because I wanted to ask about Maggie, but didn't want to incriminate her in any way.

Maggie was a friend and like a second mother to me.

"Dove?" He cocked his head.

"What?" I frowned.

"I don't like the look you're giving me. You're not hiding anything from me, are you?"

I huffed. "You know what, Dean? Dating Samantha has made you paranoid. Goodbye."

I slammed the back door as I stepped inside.

A few seconds later I heard Dean's car pull away from the house.

I don't know why it made me a little sad that he didn't stay and fight. I guess like everything else, our relationship had forever changed.

# CHAPTER 14

*I* woke up to the sound of rain hitting the roof. Mom had her shingles replaced with a tin roof a few years ago and I had no idea how much I would love the sound of rain.

After lounging in bed a few more minutes I decided to get up and get my day started. I was caught up at the quilt shop so I had the day off.

I hadn't told my mom about the call from New York. I was afraid to get my hopes up and have them dashed again. I wanted to have a few outfits ready before my deadline.

Still in my T-shirt and shorts, I grabbed a cup of coffee and curled up on the couch with my drawing pad, pencils, and my laptop.

Sipping my coffee, I finished an outfit I'd been working on last night.

After my career went up in flames in New York, I never thought I would be in the fashion industry again. But now I was thinking it might happen.

I set my pad down on the coffee table and studied my drawing.

I knew part of the reason I hadn't told Mom was because I felt guilty about being happy again. With the investigation still ongoing and Maggie one of the murder suspects, deep down I felt I shouldn't be happy about getting my career going again.

When I had first gotten the call, Mom wasn't the one I wanted to tell.

It had been Dean.

Until I remembered he was with Samantha, and I had no right to share my good news with him. It should be shared with someone you loved, and who loved you back.

For me it was my mother.

And that thought made me a little bit sad.

Elizabeth had asked me the other day when I was going to start dating again.

I told her with a murder investigation going on in Harland Creek, now was the time to think about more important things.

It made me think.

Maybe, armed with the knowledge that life was short, I should start dating again.

What could it do?

It wasn't like I was going to be getting married to them.

My cell phone beeped, and I reached for it. My hand brushed my coffee cup and knocked it over, spilling it onto my drawing.

I hissed and picked up the pad and headed into the kitchen. Thankfully it had only messed up the top drawing. I pulled it off the pad. Grabbing some paper towels, I dabbed at the drawing.

It would have to be redrawn.

I stuck the drawing on the countertop to finish drying.

Heading back to the living room, I glanced at my phone.

It was a text from Mom.

Picking it up I read her message.

"Maggie was picked up by Dean and taken to the police station for questioning. Doesn't sound good, Dove."

My stomach dropped. So much for my lazy day off.

My personal life was going to be put on hold until this investigation was done.

I headed upstairs to get dressed and head over to the police station.

## CHAPTER 15

*I* looked around the living room at the quilting ladies. It was early Tuesday morning and the day of Eleanor's funeral.

"I want to go over the list of suspects before the funeral starts. That way we can keep an eye out for anything unusual at the funeral."

Maggie glared at me but said nothing.

"Pastor John AKA Cathedral Windows. He has the most to gain by Eleanor's death. He inherits the estate and can use the money to help the church."

"Yeah, and since Eleanor cut off the money going to the missionaries, he gets to start helping with that again. I know it was near to his heart." Elizabeth nodded.

"Don't forget about the life insurance." Bertha added. "He had a nice size life insurance policy on Eleanor that he took out a few months ago."

I nodded. "That's very suspicious because he was already going to inherit upon Eleanor's death. He didn't need to take out life insurance too."

"Unless he knew he was going to kill her so he wouldn't

66

have to wait years and years before she died." Lorraine stated. "Besides, if Eleanor had control of the estate and all the money, would Pastor John even know how much money there was?"

"Good question, Lorraine. Maybe he took the life insurance out in case there was no money left to inherit."

Agnes stood up and shook her head. "I refuse to believe Pastor John killed his sister. He just doesn't have it in him."

"I understand and I agree, Agnes. All we are doing is going over all the suspects and hopefully brainstorm." I reassured her.

That seemed to soothe Agnes a bit and she sat back down.

"Let's talk about the mysterious man who knocked you down, Dove. What's his quilt block name again?" Weenie leaned forward and squinted at the board.

"Jacob's Ladder."

"That's right." She smiled.

I pointed to the suspect's name on the board. "Jacob's Ladder was seen in the sanctuary of the church. No one seems to know who he is. No leads from Dean and the pastor had no idea he'd been in the church. And he hasn't been seen since."

"Maybe he's a ghost." Sylvia added.

"If he was a ghost he wouldn't have been able to sucker punch Dove in the face." Bertha sneered.

"It wasn't exactly a sucker punch. It was more like an elbow in the face." I sighed. "I'm pretty sure he wasn't a ghost."

"I don't know, Dove." Sylvia's eyes grew wide. "My grandfather saw some weird things when he was growing up around here."

"That's because your grandfather was drunk half the time. He made moonshine." Bertha shook her head.

"He was an entrepreneur." Sylvia sat up straight in her seat.

"Let's get back to our suspects. Next up is Etta, the church secretary, AKA Bear Paw."

"My money is on her," Maggie said.

"Why?" I studied her.

"First of all Eleanor knew Etta had a crush on the pastor. It always infuriated Etta when Eleanor would tease her about it, but she was always too scared of Eleanor to stand up to her. Etta was also in charge of filling up the baptistry for baptisms. She would come in a couple hours early to do that. Maybe Eleanor was there, giving Etta a hard time and Etta snapped. Shoved her in the water and drowned her. Second, I think Etta got scared when the police interrogated her and that's why she threw Pastor John under the bus to throw suspicion off herself." Maggie nodded.

"It's certainly plausible. Don't underestimate the quiet ones." I shivered.

"Who is Confederate Rose?" Donna cocked her head. "That's a new name."

"Yes. Confederate Rose is Eleanor's interior designer. Victoria Felts. She was the one who decorated her kitchen. I ran into her when I was over at Bettie's Boutique getting some fabric..."

"Bettie's Boutique has fabric?" Elizabeth frowned. "When did they start carrying fabric?"

"They don't. Stacey got a shipment in by mistake."

"Why didn't she call me to take a look? I could use some fabric." Agnes looked a little offended.

"What's wrong with my fabric?" Mom stiffened in her seat. "I carry all the quilting fabric you could ever need."

I clapped my hands together. "Okay, okay. Let's stay on track."

"Why do you think Victoria is a suspect, Dove?" Weenie looked at me.

"She told me that Eleanor didn't finish paying her for the job she did. She said that she told Eleanor she better pay her the full amount or she would regret it. She said she always got paid. No matter what."

"Hmmm. I don't know. Killing someone because they didn't pay you? Sounds a little lean on the reasons to kill if you ask me." Sylvia sighed.

"Victoria could very well have done it. Rumor is she has an uncle in the mafia in Nevada." Maggie nodded. "She probably didn't do it herself and just put a call in to have her uncle do it."

I frowned. "How did you know about her ties to the mafia, Maggie?"

She gave me a droll look. "Honey, I'm a hairdresser. People get in my chair and I hear more confessionals and gossip than a Catholic priest."

Sylvia nodded. "It's true."

"Who else is on the list? We're going to be late for church if we don't finish this up." Mom glanced at her watch.

"Lester Hammond. AKA Arkansas Traveler. He was the one I heard threaten the pastor to make good on Eleanor's promise of fixing up the trailers in the Chateau RV Park. He even threatened Pastor John. And it's who I found out from that Pastor John had a life insurance policy out on his sister."

"It's no secret that Lester and Eleanor had a feud going for a while. He has some motive." Lorraine nodded.

The room went silent for a minute.

Maggie groaned. "Go ahead. I know it's time you all talked about me and my motive to kill the old witch. Let's get this over with."

"Fine." I swallowed. "Maggie, you're next."

"AKA Wild Goose Chase," Weenie said brightly.

"Maggie, you were caught on video slapping Eleanor the week before she died. It's common knowledge that Eleanor had been after you and Sylvia for years to sell your building to her."

"That's right. And that old bat wanted to raise the rent on everyone when she got the building too." Maggie lifted her chin.

"Slapping Eleanor isn't motive enough for killing her," Bertha said impatiently. "Can we go to the funeral now? I want to get there early and check out who brought what food."

"Well, if there's nothing else that ties Maggie to the crime then we should go." Lorraine stood.

Mom and Elizabeth shifted uncomfortably in their seats. There was no way I was outing finding Maggie's necklace in Eleanor's room.

Mom lifted her chin. "There is something else." She looked at Maggie.

Maggie looked away but said nothing.

"What?" Sylvia frowned.

"Dove found Maggie's necklace in Eleanor's room." Elizabeth stated.

All eyes were on Maggie.

"It's true. My necklace was found in her room." Maggie lifted her chin. "I had been missing it for weeks. I thought I had lost it. I had no idea Eleanor had stolen it. Which means she was in my house. I only took that necklace off before I went to bed and always put it on before I went to work."

"That means Eleanor broke into your house and stole it." Weenie shivered. "While you were sleeping."

"Or paid someone to steal it." I added.

A gasp went up around the room. There was one person in Harland Creek who had been caught breaking into people houses.

"Louie," I said.

The room went silent.

"Looks like it's getting late. We should really be going." Agnes stood and hooked her purse on her arm. "Now that we have gone over the suspect list and everything is fresh in our heads, let's keep an eye on them at the funeral."

"True. All the suspects will be there, well, all except Jacob's Ladder." Mom nodded.

As the ladies headed out of the house to get into their cars, I had a sneaky suspicion that there was more to this case than met the eye.

## CHAPTER 16

*E*veryone arrived at the funeral home for the viewing. Even though we were about ten minutes early, the parking lot was almost full. I was shocked since no one liked Eleanor. I figured all the visitors were there to pay their respects to Pastor John and not because Eleanor was the town's favorite.

I smoothed out my black pantsuit and grabbed my clutch. Mom stood beside me at the car and cocked her head at me. "You look very pretty, Dove. I don't often see you dressed up. You should do it more often."

I smiled and barked out a laugh. "Well I don't exactly have many occasions to dress up. Jeans and a T-shirt are basic attire for working in a quilt shop."

She clucked her tongue at me. "I'm not talking about the quilt shop. I'm talking about you going on a date."

"Who's going on a date?" Agnes joined us. She glanced at her green dress and then at me.

"No one is going on a date," I snorted.

"That's the truth." Mom shook her head. "Agnes, please

tell my daughter that she needs to start putting herself out there if she wants to find a husband and get married."

"Husbands are overrated." Bertha walked over and snorted. "Believe me. I've had my fill of them."

"And every one of them died." Agnes said slowly and narrowed her eyes on Bertha. "Maybe we need to open a case for each of your husbands."

Bertha glared and made her way to the front door and waited for it to open.

"What was that about?" Elizabeth walked over to us with the rest of the ladies.

Agnes held up a hand and began ticking off fingers. "We decided Dove needs to be set up on a date, so while we're inside be looking for some potential candidates..."

"Hold on!" I interjected.

Agnes held up a second finger. "While we were on the subject of husbands, it came out that Bertha has had a lot of them and maybe we should be investigating their deaths since she didn't like them so much. That's why she cut in line and is at the front."

"Typical Bertha." Lorraine shook her head.

"It is rather odd. That all her husbands died." Weenie said softly.

"Those men died because they were in bad health to begin with and she knew it. She liked them to have one foot in the grave, the other foot on a banana peel." Maggie nodded.

We all silently agreed.

The doors to the funeral home opened and people began drifting inside.

"Everyone keep your eyes and ears open to anything that we might find helpful to this case." I said softly. Everyone nodded.

Once we made it inside, we stayed in the line that led to

the pastor. When we got to the pastor we all said our sympathies and gave him a hug.

Agnes informed Pastor John that some of the ladies would slip out early from the funeral service to make sure the food in the fellowship hall was set out and ready to feed the mourners.

Maggie wandered off to speak to a couple of ladies while Sylvia and Elizabeth walked around the room greeting friends. The rest of the ladies went their own way, and I was hoping they were trying to find some kind of information to help with the case.

I spotted the dish of mints by the funeral director's office and headed over to grab one.

I took a butter mint and put it in my mouth. The candy quickly dissolved.

"Dove. You're looking better." Ben came up behind me.

I turned and smiled at him. "Yeah. I don't think it's going to scar, thanks to your attentiveness."

He narrowed his gaze on my cheek and reached out with his hand. "Let me see." His fingertips grazed my skin and suddenly I was feeling my body heat with his touch.

"I think you're right. I don't think it will leave a scar." His handsome face broke into a smile.

I cleared my throat and glanced away. "I didn't know you were back in Harland Creek. After we graduated, I thought you were headed to the University of Washington."

"I did. On a full scholarship. I ended up partying too hard and losing it. So I moved back here. My parents were real upset that I lost my scholarship."

"Wow. I had no idea. You were never the party animal in high school."

"Which is why I partied in college. All that freedom away from my family who always kept me in line." He laughed. "Anyway, once I moved back here, I ended up helping my dad in his garage and saving money. I went to night classes at the community college to be a paramedic. The plan was to save enough money to go to medical school. At the rate I'm going it may take until eternity."

"Medical school. That's quite a big undertaking." I nodded. "I can see you as a doctor."

He grinned.

My heart sped up a bit.

I glanced around the room. "There certainly are a lot of people here. I wasn't expecting so many to show up. Eleanor wasn't exactly…"

"Liked?" Ben cocked his head.

"I was going to say an easy person." I cringed. "But yes, she wasn't exactly liked."

"I'm shocked that Etta showed up." Ben nodded toward the secretary who was dabbing her eyes with a handkerchief.

I followed his gaze. "Etta? I know she didn't like Eleanor but she's the pastor's secretary. Why wouldn't she be here?"

Ben chuckled. "Because she tried to poison Eleanor. A few months ago."

My eyes widened. "She what? How?"

"She put eye drops in her coffee. Etta claimed that she thought it would just give Eleanor diarrhea but that's not how it works. It caused her blood pressure to go high and then bottom out. Eleanor passed out in the church office and Etta called 911. I was on duty that day."

"Did Eleanor press charges? Did Etta get in trouble?" Questions raced through my mind.

"Eleanor didn't press charges. I figured she wanted to hold that over Etta. You know how Eleanor was."

"Yes, I do." I knew all too well.

"I'm surprised that Pastor John didn't fire Etta."

His eyebrows shot up. "He never knew anything about it. Eleanor made us all promise not to tell him."

"That's odd. I would have figured that Eleanor would want Etta fired, after what she did."

"If Etta wasn't there, then how else could Eleanor keep tabs on what was going on at church?" He snorted and then took a mint.

"Going on?"

He shrugged. "Yeah. Pastor John had been saying how he wanted to increase our missionary budget. I don't think Eleanor wanted that. She had a say where every penny went."

"I guess she won't have a say anymore." I added.

"I guess not." He turned his full attention on me. "I'm glad to see you are back in Harland Creek, Dove. Do you plan on staying?"

"I don't know. I guess I'm still trying to figure my life out." I sighed heavily.

"While you are trying to figure things out, we should go out sometime. Have dinner and catch up." He gave me a slow grin that made my heart speed up.

I felt my face heat. "I don't know."

Dean walked over and interrupted our conversation. "Don't know about what?"

Ben turned his attention to Dean. "I was just asking Dove out."

Dean snorted. "She's too busy to date. She's too focused on herself and getting her career back."

Irritation flared in my veins. Dean had no idea what I was doing in my life or my career.

I turned to Ben and gave him a big smile. "How about Friday night?"

"Loftin's okay?" He cocked his head.

"Loftin's is perfect. I'll see you then." Ignoring Dean, I walked over to find my mom.

*A*fter the viewing, I headed over to the church to help get the food ready for after the funeral. In the South, after a funeral, there was always a big potluck. Everyone in the church had brought a dish and we laid it all out along the counter of the fellowship hall.

On the way over I told Mom about Etta poisoning Eleanor. She'd been more shocked at the fact that eye drops could be lethal and not just give someone diarrhea.

"Be careful what you say, Dove." My mom whispered to me. "There are more ladies coming in that aren't part of our detective group."

I snorted. "We're not a detective group."

"Oh yes, we are." Agnes walked through the door and narrowed her eyes at me. "We're better than Columbo."

I put the chicken casserole dish on the counter and looked at her. "Agnes, has anyone told you that you have super hearing?"

"It's not real, Dove." Bertha elbowed me aside to set the asparagus dish on the counter. "Agnes got hearing aids. She turns them up real high so she can hear everything people say."

I looked over at Agnes who glared at Bertha. "Is that true?"

She crossed her arms over her chest. "So what if it is? I'm not doing anything wrong."

"I believe it's an invasion of privacy, dear." Lorraine slipped a slice of cucumber in her mouth. "Especially when you turn them up at the doctor's office to hear other people's diagnosis. Now everyone knows that Margie Smith's husband gave her an STD."

Agnes stuck her chin in the air. "How is it my fault that her husband is a no-good cheater. She ought to divorce him and take everything."

"Or just help him die," Bertha added.

The room grew quiet and all eyes were on Bertha.

She didn't seem to mind. She went right on, setting out the plastic silverware.

I cleared my throat and looked at Agnes. "Did you discover anything at the viewing? Might as well take advantage of your super hearing."

Agnes cringed and looked around. She leaned in and spoke in a low voice. "Don't let this get around but Maggie and Lester were very chatty. I found them in the office when I went to the bathroom. They were standing close together and whispering."

"Did you hear what they were saying?"

"No. As soon as Maggie saw me she motioned for Lester to zip it. I stayed in the bathroom hoping to overhear something. I heard nothing. By the time I walked back into the office they had left."

"Maggie knows everyone. Maybe they were just talking about the case, like everyone else."

"I don't think so, Dove." Agnes glanced around the room

and then leaned closer. "Maggie and Lester couldn't stand each other. Apparently they had gotten into some kind of dispute years ago when Maggie's husband owned the garage in town. Lester used to work for him until his death. Lester wanted Maggie to sell the garage to him but under the asking price. She told him she couldn't financially do that and they fell out. When it was sold to the new owner, Lester quit and that's one reason he ended up moving to the RV park, because it's cheap. As far as I know they haven't talked since."

"That's odd they should be talking now. Maybe with Eleanor's death, they realize life is short and they are trying to forgive."

Agnes arched her brow. "Or maybe they both know more about this case than they are letting on. They are both suspects. Maybe they are trying to band together." Agnes narrowed her eyes at Bertha who was headed right in our direction.

She spoke through pursed lips. "Not a word of this to anyone. Especially Bertha."

I nodded and walked back to the refrigerator just as the line of mourners began to gather outside the door.

There were so many ladies behind the counter to help serve that I felt like I was in the way. I told Mom I would be out in the dining area, refilling tea glasses. But my real intent was to talk to Maggie or Lester.

I went from table to table, filling glasses with tea. I tried to move quicker but there was at least one person at each table enquiring about the state of my love life. I had three offers to be set up on a blind date and one offer of marriage from Mr. Miller who was at least ninety years old.

By the time I reached the table where Lester was sitting with some of his buddies I had braced myself.

"Dove, you look a little flustered." Lester frowned. "You okay?"

"Just tired of people meddling in my personal life." I grouched.

He barked out a laugh. "This is Harland Creek. You better get used to people meddling in your business." His brows knit together when one of his friends got up for seconds.

Lester looked at me. "Do you have a minute?" He pointed to the empty seat.

Shocked at my luck, I nodded enthusiastically. "Sure." I sat down and he leaned over.

"I want to apologize for what you witnessed in the grocery store. I'm not usually that upset over my roof, but the leak has gotten bigger, and nothing has been done about it."

"I'd be upset too if I was in that situation. Especially with the cooler weather that we are going to have. Wanting to have your home ready for winter is not an unrealistic expectation." I nodded.

"It's not too much to expect Pastor John to do the right thing, correct?" He leaned toward me. "That's all I'm asking. For someone to do the right thing. Lord knows, Eleanor never did." His eyes hardened as he said her name.

"Dove."

I looked up at the sound of Maggie calling my name.

"Hey, Maggie." I smiled.

"What are you doing? You're supposed to be refilling glasses." She narrowed her eyes at me and then looked at Lester. "Lester, you stop bothering Dove with all your war stories."

Lester started to say something but I guess thought better of it and slammed his mouth shut.

I quickly got to my feet and took my pitcher with me.

As I refilled glasses I noticed Maggie lingering at Lester's table. Instead of walking back to the kitchen to help, she headed for the side door that led outside. Lester waited a few seconds before following after her.

After he shut the door behind him, I went over to the window and looked out. Lester was getting into Maggie's car. They pulled out of the parking lot and left.

I made my way back to the kitchen, avoiding any more people who were trying to set me up.

"Well? You find out anything or are you out there flirting?" Bertha snorted.

"You know as well as I do there's nobody out there to flirt with." I shot her a glare and spotted Agnes by the ice machine.

I walked over to her and glanced around making sure no one was nearby.

"Here's something interesting."

"What?" Agnes's head jerked up and she gave me her full attention.

"Lester wanted to talk. He said he was sorry about getting onto Pastor John at the grocery store. I think he wanted to tell me something else but Maggie walked up."

Agnes's eyebrows shot up. "Then what happened?"

"She told Lester to quit bothering me so I could get back to work. After I walked away, she lingered at his table and then went out the side door. They left together."

She shook her head at what I had just disclosed. "I have a bad feeling, Dove."

I put my hand on her shoulder. "I know. Maybe it's time we do some investigating without Maggie knowing."

She looked up at me with sad eyes. "I think you're right. I'm afraid that things aren't what I hoped them to be." She excused herself and went to the bathroom.

I sighed. I had a bad feeling that what we were going to find at the end of this case would change the whole town forever.

"*How* do I look?" I tore my gaze from my reflection to my mom who was sitting on my bed.

"You look lovely, as always, Dove." She smiled. "That outfit is new. Where did you get it?"

I snorted. "I made it. It's some of the material that I bought from Stacey."

Mom's eyes widened. "You did a wonderful job. I don't remember ever seeing a pattern like that. Where did you get it?"

I ran my hands down the front of the light gray jumpsuit. "I made the pattern myself."

"Dove. It's beautiful."

"Thanks." I grabbed my lipstick and swiped it across my lips.

Mom stood up from the bed and walked over. She ran her hand across my sleeve. "I mean it. It's better than I've seen in stores. You should do something with this. Sell them in stores."

I bit my lip, contemplating how much to actually tell her.

Then decided to come clean. "Well, I wanted to wait until I had more drawings, but…"

"But what?" She pressed.

"I was contacted by a manufacturer. They asked if I could draw some designs for women's fashions. So that's what I've been doing. Sketching out some renderings at night so I can sew them. So far I've made this pantsuit, a wrap red dress, and that dress I was wearing when Eleanor's body was discovered."

"Why didn't you say something earlier? I could have given you more time off from the quilt shop."

"Because I like quilting. It lets my mind wander and I can think up design ideas."

"And help solve crimes." Mom winked.

"That too." I laughed and glanced at the time on my nightstand.

"I'll let you finish getting ready." Mom walked out and shut the door behind her.

Fifteen minutes later, as I was slipping into my heels, I heard the doorbell ring.

My heart sped up. I looked at my reflection. "Stop being so nervous. It's just a date. That's all. Besides it's just Ben." I grabbed my purse and headed downstairs.

I stepped into the living room and met Ben's gaze. A slow smile grew across his face.

"Wow, Dove. You look beautiful." He held my gaze.

I felt my face heat and I ducked my head and smiled. "Thank you." I looked at his dark pants and button-up shirt. "You look very handsome as well."

I didn't think it was possible but he was better looking out of his uniform.

"Shall we go?"

"Sure."

"Goodbye, Mrs. Agnew." Ben smiled at my mom.

I wasn't sure, but I thought she was blushing. Seemed like Ben had that effect on a lot of women.

The ride over to Loftin's was quick. We fell into easy conversation about the small town we'd grown up in.

He held the door for me as we walked in and pulled out my chair at the table.

It was the small things that made me miss being in a relationship.

After we ordered we sipped our drinks and talked.

"So how do you like being back in Harland Creek?" He cocked his head, his gaze totally focused on me.

"It's a little weird, I guess."

"Weird? How so?"

I fiddled with my gold bracelet. "I was perfectly happy living in New York until all that stuff happened. I don't suppose you know about all that?"

"You're talking about your partner deceiving you and moving drugs in your merchandise. And how you lost your business designing high-end children's clothes." He arched his eyebrow.

Somehow the embarrassment wasn't so overwhelming.

"Yeah." I ducked my head. "That."

"That must have been hard. Trusting someone to help you with your dreams only to have it crash around you. I'm sorry that happened to you."

I blinked and smiled. "Thank you for saying that. You're the only person who's worded it that way."

"It's hard to earn trust but once you lose it, it takes forever to rebuild it. I hope that what happened to you won't stop you from pursuing your dreams."

"I thought it had, but now I'm beginning to think I still might have a career in design." I touched the sleeve of my jumpsuit.

His gaze followed my hand. "Did you make that outfit

yourself?"

I nodded. "I did. It's an original design."

He reached over and picked up my hand. With his free hand he examined the material. "Wow, that's really good. Now I know why you did so well in New York. This is really professional."

I let out a laugh. "Thank you."

"I'm surprised to see you here." Dean sidled up to the table with Samantha at his elbow.

"Hello, Dove. Hello, Ben." Samantha gave us both bright smiles.

My stomach cringed. "Hello, Samantha. I didn't know you two were having dinner here tonight." If I had known I would have rescheduled for another night.

"Dean. Samantha. How are you?" Ben said politely but didn't stop holding my hand.

Dean narrowed his gaze at him. "I have to say I'm pretty surprised to see you two here."

"Oh yeah? Why is that?" Ben blinked. "I'm sure you over-heard us making plans for tonight."

Dean glared and then pressed a smile to his face. "I have to warn you, Ben. She's a career girl."

I glared at him while I addressed my date. "Ben, you'll have to forgive Dean. He hasn't seen me in years and has no idea what he's talking about."

Ben let go of my hand and eased back in his chair. "I think it's great that women can have both a career and a romantic life."

Dean's face went red. So did mine, but for a totally different reason.

Samantha blinked and looked between the two men, unsure how to react.

"Dove, can I speak to you for a minute?" Dean gritted his teeth.

"Sure. What's up?" I crossed my arms.

"Privately." His voice went low.

"Fine." I placed my napkin in the seat of my chair as I stood. I smiled at Ben. "I'll be right back. Why don't you tell Samantha about your plans to go to medical school?"

Dean grabbed my arm and walked me to the back of the restaurant near the bathrooms.

I spun around and looked at him. "I'm glad you're here. I needed to speak to you about Eleanor's murder."

He groaned.

I held up my hand. "Just listen. I found out that Etta tried to poison Eleanor with eye drops. She was trying to get back at her and instead of getting diarrhea, she passed out and the ambulance had to be called. Ben was the one who was on the scene."

Dean stared at me.

"Look, it's a clue. You should check it out. The last time we dismissed someone over the age of fifty, she turned out to be the murderer."

Dean took a big breath in and slowly let it out "Dove, what are you doing here?"

"What does it look like? I'm on a date. Besides, it's been a while since I had a nice steak dinner."

He parked his hands on his hips and looked at me. "Dove, you and I both know that Ben isn't your type."

"How do you know what my type is? Heck, I don't even know." I smiled and waved at Gabriella at a table.

"Listen. I know what you are doing."

I looked back at him. "You do?"

"You're here to try to make me jealous. Because I'm with Samantha."

My mouth dropped and then slammed closed. I was too stunned to speak. When I did, my words came out louder than anticipated.

"Dean Gray, are you crazy?"

A few people standing near us went silent.

"Dove, lower your voice." He warned.

"I will not. Look here. You don't have a say in what I do anymore. You never did. I will eat where I want with who I want and you aren't going to stop me." I spun on my heel and walked back to my table and sat down. Samantha went over to where Dean was standing with his hands fisted at his sides.

Ben looked at me across the table. "Are you okay?"

"Yes. Dean's usually so levelheaded. I don't know what's gotten into him." I crossed my arms.

"You don't?" Ben grinned. "It's perfectly clear. He's jealous."

I blinked and shook my head. "That's impossible. In fact, he accused me of being jealous."

Ben shrugged. "He's deflecting."

Maybe Ben was right. Maybe Dean was jealous. "If he's jealous, then why is he with Samantha?"

Ben barked out a laugh. "Because he's trying to stop thinking about you. Before you came back to town, he barely went out. At most he had two dates with Samantha. Now that you're here, he's trying to pretend he's over you."

I blinked and picked up my wine. I took a sip. "Well he certainly has an odd way of showing it."

Ben picked up my hand and brushed the back of my knuckles with a kiss. "I think Dean lost his chance. It's time for you to see what else the world has to offer."

His eyes bore into mine.

For the first time in a long time my heart fluttered in my chest.

Maybe Mom was right after all. Maybe it was time for me to find love again with someone who would never hurt me.

## CHAPTER 19

$\mathcal{I}$ was back in the quilt shop humming along to a Fleetwood Mac song while quilting on the longarm quilting machine. Since my date with Ben, he'd called two times.

I wasn't ready to get into a serious relationship, but dipping my toe back into the dating pool lifted my spirits.

Even Mom commented on the change in my demeanor.

"Dove, you have a visitor." Mom called out.

"Okay, I'll be right there." I stopped the machine, and turned my music off.

"Hey, you have a minute?" A familiar voice made my heart thump faster.

I turned to see Dean standing in the doorway. He was in his uniform and had his hands propped on his gun belt.

I arched a brow. "Did you come here to jump down my throat? I would have figured you have more important things to do, like find Eleanor's killer."

He pressed his lips into a thin line. "Dove, I didn't come to fight. I wanted to talk to you about what you told me regarding Etta."

I leaned my hip against the counter and crossed my arms over my chest. "Fine. What did you find out?"

He stepped inside the room and closed the door behind him. "I talked to Pastor John about Etta giving Eleanor eye drops. He was shocked."

"Well, of course he is. Eleanor told Etta she wouldn't tell him as long as Etta did whatever Eleanor wanted," I shrugged.

"Pastor John confronted Etta and she burst into tears and left the church." He cocked his head. "I was wondering if you had seen her."

"Of course not. I've been here all morning. Did you try her house?"

He ran his finger across the Dresden Plate quilt I had been working on. "I did. No one seemed to be home. I know she usually visits her mom in Natchez once in a while and thought maybe that's where she went."

"Sounds like a good place for you to look."

"That's the thing. I'm here to ask if you would go and talk to her."

I straightened. "Me? I have other things going on, you know. That's a long way to go. It's over a two hour drive."

"Actually it's three hours. There's some road construction." He ran his hand through his hair. "Look, I know I'm asking a lot, but I can't leave town right now with this case unsolved. You would be doing me a big favor."

"Why me?" I scowled.

"Because as much as I hate to admit it, you were some help in solving the last murder case we had in Harland Creek."

I lifted my chin. It was wonderful to finally be acknowledged.

"So what do you say?" He cocked his head.

"Can I bring someone?" I asked.

"Sure. I'd prefer it if you didn't drive that distance alone."

"What about gas money? Will you reimburse me?" I arched my brow.

"Sure. Just save the receipt." He turned and started to leave. "Oh, and Dove. Call me when you get back. I want to talk about what you find out."

I watched him leave and then picked up my phone. I went and called all the quilting ladies. One by one, they turned me down. For some reason everyone had plans for the day. I grabbed my purse and started to head out when Mom called out.

"Dove, there's a phone call for you." She held out the phone.

I grabbed it and put it to my ear. "Hello?"

"Dove? Hi, it's Samantha."

I frowned. "Samantha?"

"Yes, Samantha Vaughn. Dean told me you were taking a trip to Natchez and you needed me to ride with you."

"He did what?" I gritted my teeth. That lousy rat! The next time I saw him he was going to get an earful.

"Yes. He said that you would love to have some company. And I have to say, how generous that is of you. I mean, I know you and Dean dated and have history together."

"Samantha, that's really nice of you to offer to ride with me, but I know how busy you are at the pharmacy..."

"Oh, I have today off. The pharmacy is closed for some updating." Her cheery voice was wearing on my last nerve.

"I see." I struggled to find an excuse, any excuse, but I couldn't. "I'll have to fill up my car first. I'm almost on empty."

"No need. We'll take my car."

I clenched my jaw. "Perfect. Well, I'm at the quilt shop if you want to pick me up."

"I'm on my way." Samantha ended the call.

"Who was that, Dove?" Mom looked at me.

"My arch nemesis."

Mom looked totally confused.

"I have to head to Natchez to check out a lead for Dean. I should be back late tonight. So don't wait up." I headed outside to wait.

Five minutes later, Samantha was pulling up in her Audi.

"Of course she would own an expensive car." I muttered and climbed into the passenger's seat.

Samantha Vaughn talked the whole drive to Natchez. Before we went over to Etta's mother's house, which Dean had texted the directions, we stopped at the gas station. Samantha climbed out to pump the gas but I stopped her.

"I'll pump it. Since you were kind enough to drive." I just wanted to get out of the enclosed space and get some air.

"Oh, you're so sweet, Dove." Samantha smiled and handed me her debit card. She rattled off her pin number and then answered a text on her phone.

I climbed out and focused on picking the most expensive gas before filling up the car. I glanced over at Samantha. She was totally engrossed in sending a text. I squinted and tried to see if it was Dean she was texting but couldn't make it out.

The pump stopped. I hung up the handle and grabbed the receipt and stuck it in my pocket. I knocked on her window. She rolled the glass down and took her debit card back.

"I'm grabbing a drink. Do you want something?"

"A Diet Coke would be great. Thank you." She smiled brightly.

I hurried inside the gas station. I had missed breakfast and lunch. My stomach was violently protesting. I grabbed a Snicker's bar and a Dr. Pepper for me and a Diet Coke for Samantha. I went to the counter and paid for everything. I frowned. Maybe Samantha wouldn't let me eat in her car. It looked pretty spotless. I stood looking out the window and quickly ate my candy bar while scrolling through my texts.

One from Mom asking how the trip was going.

One from Bertha who said she could fix me up with her nephew.

And a text from Sylvia who said she was worried about Maggie.

I answered them all quickly before finishing my candy bar and heading out to the car.

I slid inside and handed the Diet Coke to Samantha.

She put her cell phone down and smiled when I handed her the soda. "Thank you."

A message popped up on her phone and she glanced at it and grinned.

I figured it was Dean sending lovey dovey messages to her like some lovesick boy.

I forced myself to look out the window and take a sip of my Dr. Pepper.

She started the engine and pulled out of the gas station and back onto the highway. "Dove, can I ask you something?"

"Sure. As long as it's not personal." I quipped.

Her eyes went wide.

I frowned. "What were you going to ask?"

"It's about Dean."

I sighed heavily. "What about Dean?"

"Why did you two break up?"

"Well, we dated in high school and graduated. I had an opportunity to go to New York to pursue my dream and he didn't want to go. He wanted to stay in Harland Creek." I shrugged.

"I see. Do you regret going to New York?" She asked quietly.

"No. I think I would have regretted it all my life if I hadn't gone. I did pretty well until my partner scammed me. And that's why I'm back in Harland Creek. Until I can get my life on track."

"So you don't plan on staying here?" She eyed me.

"No. There's really no job opportunity for a designer in a small town." I chuckled.

"What about…."

My phone rang just as she was about to finish her question.

I glanced at it and smiled when Ben's name came up. "Sorry I have to take this." I answered.

I talked to Ben until we pulled into Natchez. I finally ended the conversation and hung up.

"Was that Ben?" She grinned.

"Yes, it was. He calls a lot for someone I just had one date with."

"He really likes you, Dove. I can tell by the way he looks at you." She sighed contentedly.

"Maybe." I stuck my phone back in my purse and looked at the directions. "Etta's mother's house is the white house on the left. Right there." I pointed.

Samantha parked on the side of the street and we got out. I turned to face her. "You don't have to go in. I was going to speak to Etta myself."

"Oh, I don't mind. I would love to meet Etta's mother. She talks about her every time she comes into the pharmacy."

"She does?" I arched my brow.

"Yes. She said her mother is in good health for a woman her age. Although not long ago, Etta came in to buy some eye drops. Said her mother had really dry eyes. I was going to suggest a new eye drop that just came out." She smiled helpfully.

"Oh no. Don't do that." I held up my hand.

"Why not?" She frowned.

"Because Etta's mother is very private when it comes to her health. She doesn't like to be pitied."

Samantha frowned. "Have you met her?"

"No. Etta told me." I hooked the strap of my purse on my shoulder and headed up the stairs to the house.

I rang the doorbell and within a few seconds the door was opened. An older woman wearing a pantsuit blinked up at me. "Can I help you?"

"Yes, I'm here to see Etta. I'm Dove Agnew. From Harland Creek." I gave her my best smile.

"Harland Creek. Well you certainly are a long way from home." The old woman cracked a smile and stepped aside for me to enter.

"Hi. I'm Samantha Vaughn." Samantha shoved past me and stuck out her hand.

"I'm Sandra Miller." Mrs. Miller shook her hand and then waved us toward the living room.

The house was small but tidy. The living room boasted of original hardwood floors, antique furniture, and a small fireplace.

"Have a seat and I'll tell Etta you are here." Mrs. Miller ambled off to another room.

"It's kind of hot in here, isn't?" Samantha fanned her face.

"Mrs. Miller probably has the heat on. Anyone over the age of seventy will turn the heat on once the temperatures drop below seventy." I glanced around the room and then looked back at Samantha.

"You okay? Your face looks really red."

"I'm fine." She sat up straighter in her seat and placed her hands in her lap.

"If you say so." I stood and went over to the mantle. Picking up a photo, I smiled when I recognized a much younger Etta with her mom. Pastor John was in the background and it looked like the picture had been taken at a family gathering.

Etta entered the room and frowned when she saw us. "Dove? Samantha? What are you doing here?"

"Hi, Etta." I stood and walked over to her. "I was wondering if we could talk privately?"

She blinked, looking a bit confused. "Okay. Let's go to the kitchen." She turned and led the way.

Samantha stood to go with us but I shook my head. "Samantha, why don't you get Mrs. Miller to tell you about those lovely photos on the fireplace mantle?"

The look of disappointment was apparent on Samantha's face, but I didn't think Etta would open up with someone else in the room.

Mrs. Miller smiled and ambled over to the fireplace and began rattling off who everyone was in each picture.

I followed Etta into the kitchen and sat down at the small table. "Your mom's house is so cozy. Like a cottage in a fairy tale."

Etta chuckled. "It was my aunt's house. Mother moved in years ago after Father passed. Mother inherited the house after my aunt's death." She put the kettle on the stove and turned on the heat. She turned and looked at me. "I'm surprised to see you here, Dove. Is everything okay?"

I shifted in my seat and cleared my throat. "I'm not sure. I think we have to have a conversation that's going to be uncomfortable for both of us."

Etta pursed her lips together and said nothing as she waited for the water to boil. Once the kettle began to sing she fixed two cups of tea.

She sat the pretty yellow and green china teacup in front of me. She eased into the seat across from me and picked up her cup.

"Go ahead." She took a sip.

"I know about the eye drops, Etta."

Etta's face went white.

"Dean asked me to come and talk to you about it."

She blinked rapidly. "Does the whole town know?"

"No, no." I shook my head. "Just me and Dean."

"And the person you told you both." She dropped her gaze to the teacup. "That must have been Ben. He promised he wouldn't say anything when Eleanor said she wasn't pressing charges." Her hands trembled on the table.

I reached over and touched her hand. "I want to hear your side of the story. You put them in her tea, right?"

She nodded slowly. "I thought it would just give her a good dose of diarrhea. I had no idea it could be really harmful."

"Why did you do it?" I took a sip and watched her reaction.

She sighed heavily. "I guess I got tired of her constant bullying. She was always making snide comments about me having a crush on Pastor John. She started a rumor that I had even thrown myself at him." Her face went red at the accusation. "Can you imagine how embarrassing that is for a woman my age? I'm ten years older than him." She shook her head.

"Eleanor could be very hateful. I was at the receiving end of her vicious tongue."

Etta sighed. "I couldn't bring myself to tell Pastor John what I had done. I would have been terribly embarrassed. So Eleanor told me she would keep it between us if I agreed to get a file of Pastor John's and give it to her."

I narrowed my eyes. "What file?"

Etta shrugged. "I'm not sure. It was always kept in his desk at church, locked up. Only he had the key. I tried to pick the lock but I couldn't get it to budge. Anyway Eleanor was very angry with me when I didn't hold up my end of the bargain. She was yelling at me when Pastor John walked in."

"Then what happened?" I was literally on the edge of my seat.

"He made me leave the room. So I went to my office to begin packing up my stuff. I figured Eleanor was going to tell him about the eye drops and I would be fired." She took a sip of her tea. "After about ten minutes, I walked back to the pastor's office where they were arguing. That's when I heard Eleanor tell him she was stopping all funding for the missionaries."

"And Pastor John told her she was going to regret it if she tried," I added.

Etta nodded and sipped her tea. "Since Eleanor's death Pastor John is rarely in his office at church. He doesn't even eat at the diner anymore. And he always has lunch there."

Etta blinked and looked up at me under her lashes. "Dove, you're not going to tell your quilting ladies are you?"

"About me talking to you?"

"No, about the eye drops." She shook her head. "It's terribly embarrassing."

I smiled and squeezed her hand. "No, Etta. I'm not going to tell them about the eye drops. In fact, after all you've told me I think I can confidently mark you off the list as a suspect."

"Oh, that's good." Relief crossed her face. Then she frowned "There's a list?"

"Oh, Etta. With every crime, there's always a list." I sat back in my chair and sipped my tea.

# CHAPTER 21

*I* had gotten back to Harland Creek late that night. Samantha had dropped me off at the quilt shop so I could get my car. The drive back had been uneventful and quiet. I guess Mrs. Miller had talked Samantha to death so she was all out of words for the drive home, which was fine by me.

The next morning, I sent a text to Dean telling him what Etta had told me. When he didn't text back right away, I went about my business of refilling my coffee cup.

I was curious about what kind of file Pastor John had that Eleanor was so keen on finding. I decided that since I had an hour before the quilt shop opened, that I would go over to the church with the lock-picking kit Agnes had left and see if I could find the mysterious file.

Grabbing my purse, I headed for my car.

I made it over to the church in less than ten minutes. The parking lot was empty but I decided to park behind the church.

I walked up the stairs and tried the back door of the fellowship hall. As usual, it was unlocked. I stepped inside.

The lights were off but there was plenty of light for me to see.

I walked into the hallway where the pastor's office was located. The floors creaked under my feet, making a shiver run across my spine.

I tried the knob. It turned. I slowly opened the door and looked around.

The paneled wall and hardwood floor had not changed in all the years I had lived here. There was a large bookcase behind the desk. His chair was pushed in and his desk tidy and clean with only a Bible and hymnal sitting on top.

I walked around to the desk, pulled out the chair and sat. I tried the drawers and pulled one out. When I came to the last one, it didn't budge.

I reached into my jeans pocket and pulled out my lock-picking kit. After borrowing Agnes's for our first murder case, I went out and bought my own kit. I tried several times until it finally clicked. I pulled on the drawer and it opened.

The floor in the hallway creaked. I jerked my head up. "Hello?" I called out.

I stayed perfectly still and listened carefully.

I glanced down at the folder and then at the doorway. I picked up the folder from the locked drawer and stood. If the killer was outside the door waiting on me to come out I was going to have to come up with a plan.

I looked around the room. The only window the office had was a small stained glass window that had to be over fifty years old. Even if I broke it I didn't think I would be small enough to get outside to safety.

I hooked my purse on my shoulder and shoved the file inside. I looked around for any kind of weapon I could use to defend myself.

There was nothing there but books, Bibles, and a small lamp that looked like a bird cage.

I picked up the lamp and sighed.

I crept to the doorway and peered out. For some reason it looked darker than when I first entered.

"Hello? Is anyone there?" My voice cracked.

I heard another creak on the floor. I looked right and left to decide which way the creak had come from.

If I went right, it would lead me back the way I came in through the fellowship hall. If I went left, it would lead me through the children's Sunday school classrooms and a door that led outside.

The way left was shorter.

Tightening my hand on the birdcage I turned left and walked swiftly down the hall.

The floor creaked loudly with each step I took and suddenly I heard footsteps running behind me.

I screamed and then started running. Something or someone grabbed the strap of my purse and suddenly I was flung backward. I landed on my back, knocking the breath out of me. Suddenly there was a hooded figure all in black standing over me. I opened my mouth to scream but a gloved hand covered my nose and mouth.

I fought with all I had, clawing at his hand and trying to kick, but I suddenly got dizzy and the edges of my sight grew fuzzy.

He bent his head near my ear and hissed. "This is your last warning, Dove. Leave this case alone or your boyfriend will be next."

I struggled to stay awake but was pulled into the darkness of unconsciousness.

## CHAPTER 22

*I* pressed a hand to my aching head.

"Here, Dove, drink this." Pastor John pressed a glass of cold water into my hand.

"Dove, I really want you to come to the hospital and let us check you out." Ben shone his penlight in my eye and made me squint.

"There's no need. I didn't get hit on the head this time." I drank the cold water and was suddenly nauseated. I clutched my stomach and groaned. I spotted Dean headed my way and closed my eyes. The last thing I needed was a lecture.

"How is she?" Dean gave me a worried look while he addressed Ben. "And who found her?"

"I found her." Pastor John stepped forward. "I came in early to turn on the heat. Our older ladies have been complaining about it being cold in the sanctuary during the ladies Bible study. I headed toward my office and saw Dove laying on the floor. I called 911 and made sure she was breathing." He pulled a handkerchief out of his suit pocket and mopped his head. "I don't understand what you were doing here, Dove. Alone in the church."

Dean narrowed his eyes on me. "That's a good question. But first, how is she, Ben?"

"She's fine, as far as I can tell. We found the cloth the assailant used to knock her out and it appears to have ether on it."

"Ether?" Dean narrowed his eyes.

"Yes. I gave it to one of the cops who tagged it as evidence."

"Who uses ether? Isn't that an old drug?" I rubbed my head.

"Farmers use it in insecticides. It's used for window cleaning as well as stripping wood I believe. Also pharmacists carry it."

"Pharmacists?" I arched my brow and looked at Dean. "Maybe you should go question Samantha."

Ben snorted and then wiped his smirk away when Dean shot him a glare. "Look, if you're not going to go to the hospital then I want you to go home. I'll be over later to check on you."

"Deal." I smiled.

After Ben got up, Dean sat down on the floor next to me. "Are you okay?"

"With the exception of the worst headache I've ever had, yes. I'm fine."

"Did you get a good look at who did this?"

"No. He was wearing a hoodie."

"Do you think it was the same guy who hit you in the church?" He cocked his head.

"Maybe? He did say something this time."

Dean narrowed his eyes. "What did he say?"

"He told me to leave this case alone, or me and …people I care about will get hurt." I swallowed hard. "He'd said my boyfriend. He obviously knew me well enough to know I'd had a date with Ben."

"I see." The muscle in his jaw clenched. "I'll make sure you'll have a patrol car on your mom's street to keep an eye on things."

"Aren't you going to ask what I was doing here by myself?"

"I was hoping you'd tell me without me having to pull it out of you." He arched his brow.

I looked around, making sure no one was near enough to hear our conversation. "Etta told me that Eleanor wanted a file in Pastor John's desk. It was in a drawer that he kept locked and Etta never could get it."

"What's in the file?" Dean frowned.

"No idea. Etta didn't know either. She just said Eleanor wanted it bad enough to not press charges on Etta if she got it for her." I shook my head and looked around. "Where's my purse?" Dean waved over Sloan, one of the cops and told him to bring me my purse. He was back in a flash and handed it to me.

"It was found outside. Your keys, money, and credit cards were still inside. Nothing looked like it had been stolen." Dean said.

I looked inside. "One thing was stolen. The file."

"You picked the lock?" He narrowed his eyes.

"Sure did, and I had the file in my purse until I heard footsteps behind me." I rubbed my temple. Dean reached over and squeezed my hand. His phone rang.

He dug it out of his pocket and hit the end call. "That was Samantha. I'll have to call her back."

He gave me a little smile. "She said you two had a nice trip to Natchez. She's been begging me to take a long weekend and take her to one of the bed-and-breakfasts there. She loves historical homes."

My stomach clenched. The idea of Dean and Samantha snuggled up in a B&B made me want to throw up.

"Speaking of Natchez," I dug around in my purse. "Here's the receipt for gas."

He took it and then dug around in his wallet. He pulled out three twenties. "Here ya go. I'll let you know if we catch who did this." He stood and held out his hand to help me up.

I stood slowly and nodded goodbye to him.

As he walked away I should have felt bad for taking the gas money. But all I had to do was think about him and Samantha and it justified my actions.

# CHAPTER 23

*L*ater that day I tried going to work but felt sick to my stomach. After I told Mom what had happened she made me go home. I took some Tylenol and drank some hot lemon tea and went to bed.

I dreamed awful dreams of someone chasing me. When I turned to see who it was, it turned out to be Dean.

I woke up in a cold sweat at five o'clock in the afternoon. With the time change it was almost dark outside.

I slipped on my lounge outfit and fuzzy socks and headed downstairs. Looking out into the driveway I noticed Mom wasn't home from work yet. With me being out of the shop, she probably had some work to make up.

I went into the kitchen and dug my cell phone out and sent her a quick text.

She answered immediately and said she was stopping by the diner to pick up some dinner.

Relieved that she was okay, I went into the living room and plopped down on the couch.

Mom still had the whiteboard up in the corner with the

list of suspects written down. I went over to the board and crossed off Etta.

I studied the names left.

Pastor John, Eleanor's brother gained life insurance as well as the entire estate once Eleanor died.

Lester Hammond would 'hopefully' gain a fixed roof before winter came. That was a pretty thin MO and I figured something else was going on with him and Maggie.

Maggie would be free of Eleanor trying to bully and intimidate her into selling her building. Maggie knew if Eleanor ever got the building she would raise the rent so high Maggie and Sylvia would be forced to close up shop.

There was also interior decorator Victoria Felts. Eleanor stiffed her out of her money after completing a job for her. If the rumor was true and Victoria had connections to the mob, then they had killed for a lot less than money owed.

My eyes landed on the only suspect without a name. Jacob's Ladder.

So far he had attacked me twice. And both times in the church building. It didn't make sense. How did we always end up being in the same place at the same time?

He could have killed me. For some reason he didn't. He was just warning me.

But why?

The more I thought about it the madder I got.

I wasn't going to let someone scare me into giving up. I'd done that before and lost my career.

I wasn't planning on doing it a second time.

I was still on deadline to get some more fashion designs drawn up. I gathered my sketchpad and pencils and settled into the couch. I had four more designs to sketch. I normally took my time with my renderings but I didn't have that luxury. I had to work faster.

Ben sent a text saying he'd be over in an hour. That was perfect.

It would give me enough time to make a few more sketches while I worked this case out in my head.

## CHAPTER 24

*J* had worked late sketching more designs but still didn't finish. After finishing two complete outfits, I couldn't sketch anymore. My muse had run out. I was starting to think I wasn't going to meet my deadline.

I yawned as I waited for the coffee to stop brewing. Mom was in the kitchen setting out some buttered toast. We'd both just gotten up and it was still early when the doorbell rang.

Mom gave me a worried look as I went to answer it.

I peeked through the glass and then opened the door to Dean on the other side. "I know it's early but can I come in?"

"Sure. Mom's in the kitchen. Want some coffee?"

"Coffee would be great." He let me lead the way into the kitchen.

"Dean, you're here early. Is everything okay?" Mom poured three cups of coffee. She handed one to him.

"Thanks." He took a sip. "Actually no. I'm here to let you guys know what's going on."

"What's going on? Is it about the case?" I doctored my coffee with cream and sat down at the kitchen table next to Mom. Dean sat opposite of us.

"Yes." He looked at Mom and then me. "The members of First Baptist Church are calling a meeting today to take a vote."

"A vote on what?" I asked.

"To replace Pastor John."

"What!?" Mom gaped. "Everyone loves Pastor John. I can't believe the congregation is even thinking about this."

"They want it to be temporary. Until the case is solved." Dean took a sip of his coffee.

"Who is calling for this?" I eyed Dean.

He looked at me and grimaced.

"Dean, tell me." I shot him one of my looks.

"Maggie." He admitted.

Mom gaped.

"Maggie Rowe? The one in our quilting group?" I asked.

"Yes. She says it would best serve the community if Pastor John stepped down while the investigation is ongoing. Once the case is solved he can resume his duties as pastor."

Mom shook her head. "How could she? It's like she…."

"Doesn't believe he's innocent?" Dean cocked his head.

"This is ridiculous." I slammed my hand down on the table. "What time is the meeting?"

"Six. At First Baptist. In the sanctuary." Dean slowly stood and put his coffee cup in the sink. "Thanks for the coffee. Dove, walk me to the door?" It was more a demand than request.

I stood and walked him to the door. "Dean, you're a member of the church. Can I ask how you will be voting?"

He ran his hand through his hair. "Dove, you know I like Pastor John, just like everyone else. But this is a serious situation and it may be best for him to step down for the time being. I was also told that some members won't be coming back to church if he remains the pastor."

I blinked. "I can't believe what you're saying." I lifted my chin. "Look, I don't think Pastor John did anything to his sister."

"Do you have a better suspect? Who would benefit more from Eleanor being gone than Pastor John?"

I lifted my chin. "I think the guy who knocked me out in the church could answer that question. I think he's the murderer."

"He's disappeared like a ghost. And I can't arrest a ghost." He shook his head and headed out the door.

I shut the door behind him.

I had planned on finishing my drawings today. But after the news I just received that would have to wait.

I had to find the suspect before Pastor John lost everything.

*I* told Mom I was going to be late going into work. After I got dressed, I headed over to the S&M salon and waited until they turned the OPEN sign on.

I waited about twenty minutes until I saw Sylvia moving around inside and turning on lights. I grabbed my purse and headed inside.

I was surprised to see Victoria Felts already inside, sitting in a chair.

Sylvia seemed shocked to see me. "Dove. What are you doing here?"

"I'm here to see Maggie."

Sylvia snorted. "Well you wasted your gas money driving over here. She said she was calling out today and for me to cancel all her appointments." She pointed to Victoria who arched a brow. "Victoria had an appointment with Maggie. She has a big meeting tonight and needs her hair done."

"I appreciate you moving your clients around to work me in, Sylvia. I will certainly tip you well for picking up Maggie's slack." She flipped through a Cosmo magazine.

Sylvia gave her a tired smile. "I'm sorry she canceled last

minute, Victoria. Don't worry. Your hair will look spectacular for your open house in Greenwood."

The door jingled and a man wearing coveralls and work boots stepped inside. "Mrs. Felts. The foreman sent me over to pick up that special window cleaner."

"Glad you are getting around to those windows, Doug. They're over sixty years old. I always said the windows are the eyes of the house and we must make them sparkle." Victoria dug around in her Gucci purse. She pulled out her keys. "Look in the trunk. You'll find what you need there."

"Yes, ma'am." Doug took the keys and headed outside.

"I'm surprised you are still in Harland Creek, Victoria." I looked at the woman.

"Since I finished Eleanor's kitchen, word got out how good I am." She preened.

"Glad to hear you are getting a lot of business." I smiled and looked at Sylvia. "So do you know where Maggie is? Is she at home?"

Sylvia shrugged. "How should I know. She rarely speaks two words to me anymore."

I frowned. "But you two are best friends."

"That's what I thought. But ever since she's been talking to Lester Hammond, she's been acting weird. Distant. Not to mention it was her idea to try to get Pastor John to step down. She's not acting like herself." Sylvia's voice broke with emotion.

Doug popped back inside. "Mrs. Felts. There's nothing in your trunk. Did you forget to pick it up?"

"Of course not." She slapped the magazine down in the chair next to her and stood. "That ether is in there. You're just not looking for it." She started for the door.

I spun around and looked at Victoria. "Wait. Did you say ether?"

"Yes." Her heels clacked on the linoleum floor.

"What do you need ether for?" I asked. "You planning on knocking someone out?" I narrowed my eyes.

"What?" Victoria looked at me like I had grown a second head. "No, you poor idiot. Ether is an excellent window cleaner." She snorted and headed out to her car.

Sylvia stood next to me as we watched Victoria look in her trunk. "Mildred said the guy who attacked you in the church used ether, Dove."

"That's right."

"Do you think I need to call the police?" She bit her lip.

"Yes." I needed to find Maggie and talk to her but there was no way I was going to leave Sylvia alone with a potential killer.

Dean arrived in less than five minutes. By that time, Victoria was inside fuming about her missing ether.

"Mrs. Felts are you aware that someone attacked Dove in the church and knocked her out with ether?"

Victoria looked horrified. "No." Then it dawned on her and her reaction shifted. "Wait. You don't think I did it, do you?" She gaped.

"Where were you two days ago?"

"I had checked on the house in Greenwood and realized I needed something heavy to clean those windows so I drove to Starkville. Then I stopped at the grocery store." She lifted her chin. "So you see, I was nowhere near the church." She shoved her finger in my direction.

"And you just now noticed the ether was missing?"

"Yes." She crossed her arms. "Now if you don't mind, I need Sylvia to do my hair. I have a lot to do before my dinner conference tonight."

Dean nodded and grabbed my arm, leading me out the door.

Outside, I turned and looked at him. "Do you believe her?"

"I certainly don't trust her. She's had some shady connections with people in Nevada." Dean narrowed his eyes at me. "Does she look like the person who attacked you?"

I shook my head. "No. It was definitely a man. Maybe she paid someone to do it."

"It just doesn't fit, Dove." He shoved his hands in his pockets and studied the ground.

"I know." There was a lot that didn't fit about this case. We'd been digging into Eleanor's background and had a list of suspects and I felt like I was missing something.

His cell phone rang. He looked at it but didn't answer. Instead he stuck it back in his pocket.

"That wasn't official business, I take it."

He shifted his weight. "No."

I frowned. "Is everything okay?"

"It was Samantha. She wants to go out tonight but I can't. She doesn't seem to understand about my odd working hours." He glanced away.

I slapped him on the shoulder. "Don't worry. I'm going to help solve this case and when I do, you'll have all that free time to go out with Samantha."

I didn't wait for a response, instead I hurried to my car and got inside.

I had to find Maggie and get the truth out of her once and for all.

# CHAPTER 26

I drove to Maggie's house but no one answered the door when I knocked. Her car was gone so I thought I would try my other suspect, Lester.

I drove over to the Chateau RV park. When I entered I was surprised that the place looked worse than ever. Before Eleanor bought it, Gertrude Brown owned it. At least Gertrude kept the place up even though she charged an arm and a leg and no one liked her.

I found Lester's trailer and parked right in front. I noticed his truck was there so I hurried up to the door and knocked.

He answered immediately. His face fell when he saw me.

"Expecting someone else?" I asked.

"Yes, actually. How did you know?" He frowned.

I walked past him inside.

"I don't have time for company, Dove." He narrowed his eyes.

I looked around his sparse trailer. Even though he lived alone, everything was neat and orderly. The Quilt of Valor was neatly folded and placed on the back of the plaid sofa. The recliner had a single pillow with a flag embroidered across it. The carpet was freshly cleaned, and the kitchen smelled of Pine-Sol.

The TV was playing an old black and white movie with Cary Grant.

"Mind if I sit down?"

He sighed. "I'm not sure I have much choice."

I took that as a yes and sat on the sofa. He sat in the recliner.

"I need to know what's going on with you and Maggie." I held his gaze.

"I don't know what you are talking about." He avoided my gaze and fiddled with the TV remote.

"You two left Eleanor's funeral together." I leaned forward in my seat.

His eyes got wide.

"Can you tell me why? Or I can ask Dean to come over and question you."

He shook his head. "No, don't do that." He stood and walked over to the window. "Maggie was taking me over to Eleanor's house."

I frowned. "For what?"

A pained looked crossed his face. "It's not what you think. I had told her about a letter that I sent Eleanor a few weeks before her death."

"What kind of letter?"

He ran his hand across his face. "Not a good letter. I was so mad that she still hadn't fixed my roof." He pointed up to a dark spot on the ceiling. "And well, my temper got the best of me. I sent her a letter threatening her if she didn't fix it."

"You threatened her?" I stood, feeling uneasy about this whole situation.

"I was just bluffing. I wouldn't harm that old bat." He let out a breath. "Anyway, I told Maggie about it, after half the town saw me yell at the pastor in the grocery store. She said I needed to get that letter back before the police found it and tried to pin the murder on me."

"So you went to her house. Did you get it back?"

"No one was supposed to be there. That's why Maggie suggested I leave before the funeral was over. She knew all the congregation would be rallying around Pastor John and extending their sympathies." He walked back and sat in his chair. "Anyway, we got to the house and as soon as we started upstairs to her bedroom, we heard noises."

"Noises?"

"Footsteps." Lester shook his head and his face paled. "Maggie called out, asking who was there."

"And what happened?"

"We heard a deep voice."

"What did it say?"

"Leave!" He rubbed his forehead with his hand. "We were so scared, we ran out of there and back to the church where I got my truck."

"Who do you think it was?"

He turned and faced me, giving me his full attention. "Honestly? I think it was Eleanor's ghost."

I started to grin but stopped. The look on Lester's face told me he was serious.

"I still need to talk to Maggie."

A worried look came across his face. "She should have been here an hour ago. She's never one to be late. Let me call her cell phone." He went over to the kitchen and picked up his phone. He entered her number and held it to his ear. When Maggie didn't answer he looked at me with worry in his eyes. "That's not like Maggie. She always picks up when I call."

"Lester I need to ask you something and I want you to tell me the truth."

"Okay."

"Did you kill Eleanor?"

His eyes widened in disbelief. "Absolutely not. I might have hated the woman but I didn't kill her." His eyes filled with sadness. "I saw enough death when I was in the military. I can't handle any more."

I nodded. "I believe you."

Relief filled his eyes.

"But I'm starting to worry where Maggie is."

"Me too."

I looked at him and headed to the door. "You stay here in case she shows up."

He frowned. "What are you going to do?"

"I'm going to find her." I shut the door behind me.

## CHAPTER 27

"Dean, Lester is innocent. And so is Etta." I held the phone to my ear as I drove back to Maggie's house.

"Yeah, I ruled them both out a while ago. And Victoria didn't do it either. It seems we found a fingerprint on her trunk that didn't belong to her or Doug. I'm running it through the system now to see who it belongs to."

"Someone did steal her ether."

"So it would seem." He admitted.

"I kind of thought she was the killer, but her motive wasn't strong enough," I stated.

"True. So that leaves Maggie, Pastor John, and the stranger in the church who attacked you."

"Maggie called out today and told Sylvia to cancel all her appointments. I checked her home but her car wasn't there. Then I rode out to Lester's but he hadn't seen her. Dean, Lester is pretty worried about Maggie," I admitted.

"So is Sylvia. She broke down after I talked to Victoria about the ether."

"Please don't tell me you think Maggie is the killer."

"I didn't say that. I just said we narrowed down the list." Dean's voice was eerily calm.

"My money is on the stranger who attacked me."

"The question is, if he's the killer why would he stick around in town?"

"What do you mean?" I frowned and turned down the street leading to Maggie's house.

"He attacked you that first night in the church, after he killed Eleanor. And then nearly a week later he attacked you again in the church. He attacks twice and there's no eyewitness who sees him. It's like he's a ghost."

A shiver ran down my spine at Dean's words.

A ghost.

"Yeah. You're right."

"Dove, what are you thinking?" He asked.

"Meet me at the church. I have a theory." I hung up without waiting for a reply. I slowed down when I approached Maggie's house. But when I didn't see her car parked in front, I kept driving. Maggie wouldn't be at her home.

She would be at the church.

# CHAPTER 28

*I* smiled when I saw that Dean had beat me to the church. I climbed out of my car and walked over to his car.

The loud bark of a dog scared me, and I jumped back.

"Easy, Tarzan," He commanded.

"I didn't realize you had the beast with you."

"I had a hunch to bring him along. I think he can help." He gave the dog a scratch behind the ears. The dog looked up at him with adoring eyes.

"As long as he doesn't bite me." I gave the dog a warning look.

Tarzan barked. I jumped.

Dean laughed. "Come on. Let's go inside." He led the way up the steps to the front door of the church. He opened the door and went in first.

I walked in behind him and reached for the light switch. He grabbed my hand and shook his head.

"Keep the lights off," he whispered.

I nodded and stayed close behind him.

Tarzan walked up and down the rows of pews, sniffing

and then resniffing areas. When we reached the offering table, Tarzan sat down and looked up at us.

I looked at Dean. "Well? What's he doing?"

"He's done."

"That's it? Isn't he supposed to lead us to a clue or something?" I glanced from him to the dog.

"It doesn't work like that. He's a police dog. Not a bloodhound."

"Then why did you bring him?" I huffed.

"Because he gets lonely without me." Dean frowned. "Besides, he's on duty. He has to be here."

"I should have come alone." I shook my head and walked past him toward the fellowship hall.

"Wait! Let me go first." He grabbed my arm and glared. "You know, I hate it when you put yourself in danger like this."

"Oh, my gosh. I'm not a child, Dean."

"I know that! You think I don't know that!" He stared at me hard.

Anger flooded my veins and I fisted my hands at my sides. "We're not together. You shouldn't even care enough to try to protect me."

"I'll always care about you, Dove. Don't you know that?" He pulled me close and suddenly his hands were on my hips and in my hair pulling me close. Then his warm lips were on mine.

I don't know if it was because I was so stunned, or if I really wanted him to kiss me, but I leaned into his embrace.

The fact that we were kissing in a church quickly faded away.

Kissing Dean was like coming home, where everything fit and made sense.

My foggy brain started to clear, and I pressed my hand to his chest until he broke the kiss.

"Dove," he whispered.

"Dean." I swallowed and took a step back. "You are with Samantha. As much as she irritates me, I can't do that to her."

Pain etched into his eyes as he comprehended my words. I opened my mouth to say more but Tarzan started barking down the Sunday school hallway.

Dean frowned and headed down the hallway. I followed behind him.

We stopped at the end of the hallway where there was a closet.

Dean reached for his gun and pushed me behind him. "Stay there." He looked at his dog. "Tarzan, sit."

The dog obeyed and sat.

With one hand on his gun and the other on the doorknob, he turned. The door opened. Dean flipped the light switch.

I stepped closer and frowned. "It's just a closet where they keep the cleaning supplies."

Tarzan began barking at the closet.

"What's going on with him?" I stepped back, afraid the dog was broken.

Dean holstered his gun and began pulling stuff out of the closet.

"What are you doing?"

"I'm looking." He placed the vacuum cleaner by the door.

"For what?" He took a step back as he piled cleaning supplies on the floor. "Toilet paper?"

"No." He stepped inside the now-empty closet and knocked on the back wall of the closet. The expression on his face changed and he began feeling around on the wall. The plywood of the wall shook a little. He took out his pocket knife and ran it along the seam of the wood.

The wall gave way to a small opening big enough for a person to climb through.

He turned and looked at me and smiled.

"What in the world is that?"

"Hand me that flashlight." He pointed to the floor.

I grabbed it and handed it to him.

He knelt and looked inside.

"What do you see?"

"There's a sleeping bag and a camping lantern." He turned and looked at me. "That's why we can't find the murderer. He didn't leave town. He's been here the whole time. Sleeping at the crime scene."

I frowned. "It really is the guy who attacked me that first night."

Dean nodded. "Right under our nose."

Tarzan started barking and we both turned.

"What's going on in here?" Pastor John eyed us suspiciously.

"What are you doing here, Pastor John?" Dean cocked his head.

"Well, I...," he swallowed hard.

"And why are you wearing all black?" I asked. My stomach clenched.

"I saw Dean's car parked outside. I was concerned so I came over to look."

"Dressed in a black hoodie? For as long as I have known you, I've never seen you wear a hoodie."

He lifted his head. "I was going for a run."

Dean narrowed his eyes. "You run? Since when?"

"Since recently. I noticed it helps with my anxiety." He admitted.

"Admit it. You're the one who hit Dove." Dean rested his hand on his gun.

"What? No!" Pastor John shook his head.

"Dean, why would Pastor John hit me?"

"Dove, describe the build of the guy who elbowed you in the church." Dean never took his eyes off Pastor John.

"Tall and lanky."

"Just like Pastor John." Dean cocked his head.

Pastor John gaped at the accusation.

"Pastor John, I'm going to need you to come down to the police station." Dean narrowed his eyes.

"But I can't. Not right now. I have… obligations." His breathing increased.

"It can wait."

I grabbed Dean's arm. "Dean, surely you don't think Pastor John is a murderer."

Dean glared at me.

Apparently Pastor John saw an opening. He sprinted out of the hallway.

"Stop!" Dean called out. He went after him with Tarzan at his heels. "Tarzan."

"Dean, stop!" I yelled.

Dean glared at me. "He's getting away."

"No, he's not. He has nowhere to go. He's just going to run home. Let me go instead. Let me talk to him."

Dean looked at me like I was insane. "He's a killer, Dove."

I grabbed his face between my hands. "Dean, if you have ever trusted me, please trust me on this. I don't think he's the killer. But I do think he knows who it is. You have got to let me go so I can talk to him. Please."

A myriad of emotions played across his face. Anger. Fear. Uncertainty. Love.

I want to believe it was the last emotion that allowed him to let me go.

*I* ran after Pastor John before Dean could stop me. I followed him to his house. He was fast and was already up the stairs and inside the house before I was across the street. I tried the door but it was locked.

I pressed my face to the window and peered inside.

It was dark but I could see movement inside the house.

I glanced over my shoulder. Dean and Tarzan were running toward me.

I knew I had to get inside the house and talk to Pastor John before Dean got to him.

I raced around to the back of the house and tried the back door leading into the kitchen. It turned. I hurried inside and locked the door behind me.

I heard voices upstairs. Pastor John was not alone.

Dean banged on the kitchen door, but I ignored him. I ran up the stairs, following the sound of voices. Maggie stepped out of Eleanor's room and propped her hands on her hips.

"Maggie? What are you doing here?"

"I could ask the same of you." She stared hard at me.

128

"Maggie I need to talk to Pastor John. I want to help him."

"No one can help him. Only God." She shook her head and a look of sadness washed over her face.

Her words chilled me to the bone.

"I need to talk to him." I tried to walk past her, but she stepped in front of me, blocking me.

"Dove, I can't let you do that." Maggie lifted her chin.

"But you're the one who was calling for a vote to make the pastor step down. Why are you acting so protective of him now?" I glared.

"Where's Pastor John?" Dean was behind me with Tarzan at his side. "Maggie, if you don't get out of the way, I'm going to arrest you for obstructing an investigation."

"I'm right here." Pastor John stepped out of Eleanor's room. He gave Maggie a sympathetic smile.

"I'm going to need you to come with me to the police station." Dean stated. Tarzan growled.

"Dean, you can't do that. I won't let you. You're going to have to arrest me too." Maggie lifted her chin.

"Maggie," Dean warned.

"I'm serious. If you arrest Pastor John, then I want to be arrested too." She held out her hands. "Cuff me and shove me in the back of the police car."

"I can't do that, Maggie." Dean shook his head.

"Because Tarzan sits in the back. I was just going to put Pastor John up front with me. There's not enough room for two suspects." He glared.

"Wait. I have a question." I looked from Pastor John to Maggie. "Pastor John, you could have jumped in your car and driven away. It's not that far from the interstate and you could have been to Tennessee within a few hours. But you didn't."

Maggie studied the floor.

"And I think I know why." I crossed my arms over my

chest. "You came back here to protect the real killer who is hiding in Eleanor's room. And he's been the same one who was living in the church who hit me the night I was in the church."

Dean blinked and looked at Pastor John. "Is that true?"

"It's not what you think, Dean." Maggie stated. "There is more to this story than you know."

"I'm sure there is, but unless someone starts talking now, I'm arresting everyone. Including Dove."

I spun around and gaped. "Me? Why would you arrest me?"

"Because you locked me out of the house." He glared.

"How did you get in, anyway?"

"I picked the lock." He looked at Pastor John. "Someone needs to start talking."

"Maggie, why did you want the congregation to vote for the pastor to step down?" I looked at her.

"Because she thinks I really did kill Eleanor." Pastor John shook his head.

All eyes were on her. She sighed. "Yes. I did think you killed Eleanor. I figured if I could get the congregation to vote for you to step down then you would go on the run. Maybe cross the border in Mexico or Canada and live out your life anonymously."

"So you really were trying to help the pastor." I smiled.

"Of course. He's been the best pastor this town has ever had and I don't want him to go to jail." Maggie pursed her lips.

"But I didn't kill Eleanor," Pastor John pleaded.

"No, you didn't," I agreed. "But I think I know who did."

"Who?" Dean blinked and looked at me.

"The guy in black, who was at the church and I suspect is now living somewhere in this house." I looked around. "Perhaps Eleanor's room?"

"He didn't mean it." Pastor John held his hands up. "It was an accident."

Suddenly a tall lanky figure walked out of Eleanor's bedroom and stepped into the hallway. Dean reached for his gun, but I held out my hand. "Hang on."

"Who are you?"

He lifted his head and I saw familiar sad eyes looking at me. "I'm Peter. Peter Gallows. Eleanor's son."

*I* blinked. "But I didn't know Eleanor had a son."

"No one did." Pastor John wrapped his arm around the young man. "This was almost thirty years ago and it wasn't socially acceptable to be an unwed mother at that time and our father was a proud man." Pastor John took a deep breath. "So our father sent Eleanor away to New York."

"I remember that," Maggie gaped. "We were told Eleanor went to help her dying cousin."

"Our father lied. When Eleanor came back he made her swear not to ever tell a soul. He told her if she did, she would be written out of the will."

"So she kept her secret." I looked at Peter. "Until you showed up."

Silent tears ran down his face. Peter was about my age. I'd never seen someone look so hopeless.

"It was an accident. I promise." He rubbed his arm across his eyes. "I found out six months ago that I was adopted. My parents were missionaries. They lived overseas until about a month ago when they were told their funding was getting cut. So they came back to the states."

"Missionaries? The same missionaries that our church supports?" Maggie asked.

"The same missionaries that Eleanor cut the funding to." I added.

He slowly nodded his head.

"Did you know you were adopted?" I asked.

"I found out my last year in high school. My parents told me." He gave a ghost of a smile. "I was shocked, to be honest. To know they were not my biological parents was jarring. But they knew I was going off to college and they were going back into the missionary field after Christmas, and wanted me to know in case anything happened."

"Did you look for your parents?" I asked.

"No. Not until about a month ago when my parents came back to the states. I overheard them talking one night about me being the reason why their funding had gotten cut."

"Did they know that Eleanor was your mother?" Maggie asked.

He nodded. "Yes. They finally showed me the adoption papers they had in New York and it listed the mother as Eleanor Simmons. The father wasn't listed."

"So you decided to track her down?"

"Yes. Wouldn't you?" He gave me a pained look. "After all my parents had done, why would Eleanor be so cruel to cut their funding? It didn't make sense. I hired a private detective and he tracked Eleanor here."

Dean studied Peter. "What was your intent when you finally met Eleanor?"

He shrugged. "Ask her why she cut my parents' funding. It never really crossed my mind to ask why she gave me up. I mean, I'm glad she did. I have the best parents in the world."

"So what happened?" I asked.

"I came here, to the house to talk to her. I was hoping

once she saw me face-to-face, she would have some compassion and reinstate my parents' funding."

"How did the meeting go?"

Peter snorted. "She wouldn't let me in the door. When I told her I was her son, she slammed the door in my face and wouldn't talk. So I walked over to the church, hoping to talk to Pastor John…"

"You can call me Uncle John." The pastor wrapped his arm around his shoulder and gave him a reassuring smile.

Pastor John looked at us. "Peter came over. I was stunned, to say the least, when I met him. We talked and I was shocked at Eleanor's behavior. I told him I would talk to her and try to reason with her."

"Then what happened?" Dean asked.

"Eleanor refused to see reason. I had hoped that she would grow gentler in her old age, but she never did."

I looked at Peter. "How long did you stay here in Harland Creek?"

"Just for that day. Afterwards I drove to Jackson and got a hotel. I was trying to clear my head as to what to do next. I called Pastor John, er, I mean Uncle John, but his secretary told me that he was out for the rest of the day but he would be back in early the next morning due to a baptism at eight in the morning."

"So I ended up driving back that night and sleeping in my car. I parked in the back. I was awakened around four that morning by someone going in the back door of the church. So I went in. Only a few lights were on, but I recognized Eleanor in the dim light. I told her I only wanted to talk. She accused me of wanting to blackmail her into giving me money. She said she'd never give me one red cent even if I was related by blood." His voice cracked on the last word.

"So how did Eleanor end up in the baptistry?" I asked.

"She told me to leave and never come back. She said if I

ever told a soul she was my mother she would destroy my parents."

"Why that old witch." Maggie stomped her foot. "Pastor John I know she was your sister, but she was a wicked woman and I'm not sorry for saying it."

Pastor John gave her a slight smile. "I won't ask you to, Maggie."

All eyes turned on Peter to finish the story. "Anyway, she walked off toward the baptistry. She was at the top of the steps and flipped the switch to stop the water. I walked up a step or two to beg her to reinstate the funding for my parents. I told her I wasn't asking anything for myself and if she would do this, I would never return."

Peter shook his head. "I'll never forget the look in her eyes. She turned and faced me, looking down from the baptistry and told me she would destroy everything I ever loved if I didn't leave that second. I was so angry. I'd never been that angry in my life. My parents are good people and have done amazing things. In that moment, all I wanted to do was protect them. I was so angry. I walked up another step and shoved her into the baptistry."

"Did you hold her under?" Dean asked.

"No! I didn't." I left after that and went over to the house to tell Uncle John what she'd said."

"That's true. Don't you see it was an accident?" Pastor John pleaded.

Dean blew out a slow breath. "First we need to go down to the police station and fill out a proper report. Are you willing to do that Peter?"

"Yes, sir." He nodded.

"You can't charge him with murder, Dean."

"Dove, don't." He warned.

"She's right. You can't." Maggie lifted her chin.

"Everyone needs to calm down." Dean looked at the pastor. "Can you follow us to the station?"

"Of course. Let me get my keys." The pastor went down the hallway to his room.

"Are you going to cuff me?" Peter asked.

"I don't think that's necessary." Dean looked at me. "You ride with me, Dove."

I frowned. "But I thought there wasn't enough room with Tarzan."

"You'll have to sit with him."

I gaped. "In the back?"

"Yes, Dove. You should get along well with him. Petunia is crazy about you."

I glared as we walked out of the house with Peter. "That's different. Petunia's a goat."

Peter gave me an odd look. "You have a pet goat?"

I sighed. "I'll explain on the way to the police station."

*I* sat as close to the door as possible.

"How's it going back there?" Dean looked at me in the mirror.

"Can you hurry up? I don't think he likes me." I held my breath as Tarzan dug his snout in my neck and sniffed. "I think he's getting ready to bite."

Dean laughed. "He's just getting to know you."

"I would prefer getting to know him over a cup of coffee, not his teeth near my neck." I closed my eyes and tried to think of anything to calm my racing heart.

"Peter, I have a question." I said.

"Okay."

"Why did you stay after Eleanor was found dead?" I looked at Dean in the rearview mirror.

"Because I felt bad that she died. I mean, after I pushed her in the baptistry, she stood up and screamed at me. I had no idea she slipped again."

"Wait." Dean looked at Peter. "She stood up after she was pushed?"

"Yes." Peter nodded. "She was okay after I left."

"Why were you in the church that night when me and the ladies were in to have a look around?"

His shoulders slumped. "I went into the church to pray for forgiveness. I fell asleep on the pew. It wasn't until I heard voices that I got scared. I'm really sorry about elbowing you, Dove." He turned in his seat to look at me. "I hope I didn't do any real damage."

"I'm fine." I gave him a reassuring smile. "No scar at all."

"But you stayed in Pastor John's house. You could have left." Dean stated.

"I wanted to make sure Pastor John didn't go to prison for something he didn't do. I kept hearing the rumors about the different suspects and I couldn't in good conscience leave town and have someone else go to jail in my place. But Pastor John still wouldn't let me go to the police. He said he was sure the investigation would rule her death an accident." He shook his head. "I'm sorry. I should have come forward sooner. Now everything is a mess."

I frowned. "Where's the file?"

Peter looked over his shoulder at me. "What file?"

"The file that you took from me the second time we had a run-in at the church." I slowly pushed Tarzan away from me.

"What file? I don't have a file." He frowned and shook his head. "I only saw you once at church."

"We found a hiding place in one of the closets where someone had been staying."

He shook his head. "That wasn't me. I stayed at Pastor John's house."

"So you didn't attack me in the church with a rag filled with ether?" I leaned forward in my seat.

His eyes grew wide. "Absolutely not. Why would I do that?"

I sat back in my seat. "Dean, turn around."

"What?"

"Peter is telling the truth. He wasn't the one who attacked me the second time in the church. That person was after whatever was in that file. And that person is probably going back to the church now that no one is watching the church."

"Why are they going back into the church?" Dean frowned and slowed the car.

"Because the file they got is the wrong one. When I heard footsteps in the church that day, I switched out the files in case something happened to me."

Dean's eyes widened. "Why didn't you tell me that day?"

"Because I wanted to see if the killer would notice and come back. And I can guarantee you that the murderer is there now trying to find out where I hid the real file. Besides, the autopsy report said Eleanor drowned. Which means she was alive when she was in the water, breathing. Someone held her down."

Peter gasped. "But why?"

Dean's phone dinged. He glanced down at the text.

"Who is it?"

"The fingerprint from Victoria's trunk came back with a match." He looked at Peter. "And it's not you."

Dean made a U-turn and sped back in the direction of the church.

"Where are we going?" Peter asked.

"I think we are about to find out who the real killer is."

## CHAPTER 32

$\mathcal{W}$e parked away from the church in case the murderer was watching.

"Stay here." Dean ordered Peter. And then he turned to look at me. "I would say stay here to you but I know how well you listen."

I brightened and slid out of the car when he opened the door.

Tarzan walked between us as we headed for the church.

"We'll go in the side door. Stay behind me and stay quiet."

"I know the routine." I glared.

He didn't say anything else but shot me a glare.

Dean went in first with Tarzan and I followed.

We headed for the office just as a figure stepped out.

I blinked and frowned. "Ben? What are you doing here?"

"Dove. I could ask the same." His eyes flickered to Dean and hardened.

Dean rested his hand on his firearm. "Hands in the air, Ben."

"What are you doing? It's Ben. He's here…" I looked at him. "Why are you here, Ben?"

Ben swallowed.

"He's here to get the file, Dove." Dean stated. "The finger-prints on the trunk of Victoria's car came back to match Ben. Anytime someone goes into the medical field they are required to get fingerprints. That's why he was in the system."

I blinked in disbelief. "But why?"

"Because Ben wanted the last paper trail that said Eleanor had a son. Isn't that right, Ben?"

Ben straightened his shoulders. "You can't go around accusing people of crimes. I want to speak to an attorney."

"I'm sure you do." Dean smirked. "Want to tell Dove the truth or do you want me to?"

Ben blinked and looked at me.

"Why don't you tell me, Ben?" I glared at him.

When he said nothing, Dean spoke. "Ben wants the file so no one finds out who Eleanor's son is."

"But we already know it's Peter." I shook my head.

"Is it?" Dean cocked his head at Ben. "During that time, there were a lot of adoptions from the agency that Peter was adopted through. There was a report not too long ago, that babies were accidently swapped at birth. And I remember when Ben's father needed a kidney transplant, all the family was tested. Even Ben. And Ben wasn't a match because he was adopted."

I looked at the man who'd taken me on a date and shiv-ered. "Ben, you wanted the file because you found out that Eleanor was *your* mother. How did you find that out?"

Ben swallowed.

"Tell me." I demanded.

"Eleanor was diabetic. She often called me when she needed to have some blood samples taken for her doctor. She hated going to the doctor because she didn't want anyone to know she was in bad health so she got him to agree to let me draw her blood and take it in for her. One day as I was drawing her blood I saw an envelope from the adoption agency in New York. The same one I had been adopted from. I asked her about it but she said it was none of my business."

He shook his head. "I decided to do a DNA test on a sample of her blood that day. I didn't really expect much, but when it came back she was my mother I was floored. Every time I saw her after that I couldn't help but want to tell her. I even brought her flowers with my next visit and you know what she did? She accused me of trying to seduce her for her money!" He snorted. "Can you believe that? One day I was in the closet at church looking for some paper towels to put in the men's bathroom and I came across that small hiding spot. I don't know what urged me, but I crawled inside and sat. Etta and Eleanor were in the pastor's office and I could hear everything they were saying. I heard Eleanor threaten to press charges on Etta if she didn't find that file from New York and give it to her.

I knew that it contained everything to prove Eleanor was my mother."

"So what happened on the morning of her murder?" I asked.

"I was already in the sanctuary waiting on Eleanor. I was supposed to drop-off her insulin at the house, but I wanted to talk to her about what I knew."

"Insulin?" I blinked.

"Yes, Eleanor was a diabetic. She did her best to hide it from the community. And her drinking did her no favors. Anyway, I heard voices and realized she was not alone, so I ducked down and hid. I saw her arguing with a guy my age. When she told him that if he told anyone that she was his mother, she would destroy everything he cared about, something in me broke. I realized what a monster she was. I drew up a syringe of insulin." Ben's eyes glazed over.

"Then what happened?" I clasped my hands at my sides.

"He shoved her in the baptistry and ran out. I saw her stand up. I walked over to the steps of the baptistry as she was crawling out and I started laughing at her. She was furious and started cursing at me right here in the church. I couldn't believe it. I told her that I knew who she was. That she was really my mother. She said she cursed the day I was born. She slipped on the step and hit her head. She was still conscious when I shot her up with insulin and then put her back into the baptistry to drown."

"That's why the autopsy report said she drowned. She was still breathing but in a diabetic coma from the insulin." Dean finished.

Ben nodded. "I'm impressed, Dean. I didn't think you were that smart. I mean after all you let Dove go." His eyes drifted over to me.

"You were the one who attacked me with the ether." I narrowed my eyes at him.

"Yes. I saw that interior decorator had it in her trunk when I was at the grocery store. It was easy enough to steal. All I had to do was offer to load her groceries for her."

"What's going on?" Peter appeared behind us. Dean and I turned and as soon as we did Ben grabbed me. He pressed a syringe to my neck.

"I'm sorry, Dove. I really did like you. I could have seen a future for us. But I'm not going to prison. This is a paralytic. Once I inject it you'll stop breathing. And I guess you can tell what comes next." He tightened his arm around my neck as he held me like a shield between him and Dean.

Dean had his gun in his hand and was aiming for Ben. Tarzan growled. "Let her go."

Ben eased back to the door leading outside. "I can't do that. You just let us go and I won't hurt her."

"You're not walking out of here." Dean spat out.

"If you love her, you'll let us go." Ben pressed his mouth next to my ear.

Fear filled my entire body and I felt like I was going to pass out. It was all I could do to stay on my feet.

Ben reached back for the doorknob and turned. The door opened.

I knew once I was in a car with Ben, I wasn't ever coming back.

"Ben, please. Don't do this." I pleaded. Tears stung my eyes.

"Shut up." He tightened his grip.

Stars swam before my eyes. I felt myself walking backwards down the steps. Every step we made back, Dean inched forward.

We were outside and I was being dragged backwards. I strained to keep my neck away from the syringe, but he kept it close enough to draw blood. I swiped at my neck and pulled back my hand.

"I don't feel good." My stomach turned at the smear of blood on my palm.

"Just a little more to go until we get to the car." He stepped backward.

Dean screamed a command at Tarzan who leapt off the steps and lunged toward Ben. I cringed waiting to feel the sharp bite of the dog's teeth but was shoved to the ground.

Tarzan bit down on Ben's thigh. Ben let out a scream. Dean was on Ben and had him cuffed before he called Tarzan off him.

Peter ran over to me and helped me sit up. "Are you okay?"

"Yes. I just faint at the sight of blood." I held up my hand for him to see.

He took the hem of his shirt and cleaned off my hand and helped me stand. Before we got into the car, people were pulling up to the church to see all the commotion. All the quilting ladies were there with my mom, and even Samantha pulled up asking questions. Half the town had shown up.

Should have figured. There are no secrets in a small town.

Dean put Ben in the car and Tarzan in the front with him. He then walked over to me and cupped my face. "Are you okay?"

"Yes."

"Let me see your neck." He gently turned my face and examined where the needle had punched my skin.

My eyes met Samantha's. I expected to see anger or jealousy. But all I saw was sadness.

"I'm fine, Dean." I pulled away. "You need to get Ben to the station."

He nodded.

No sooner had he left than the Harland Creek Mystery Quilters descended on me for answers.

"*J*'m so sorry, Maggie. I can't believe I thought you had killed Eleanor. Can you please forgive me?" Sylvia sobbed.

"Of course, you old bird." Maggie pulled her into a hug. "You're my best friend."

"Anyone else want some tea?" Mom held up the teapot.

"None for me. I'll be up half the night on the toilet." Agnes gruffed.

"Agnes, nobody wants to hear about your bladder." Bertha scowled.

"Well nobody wants to hear about your hammertoe." Agnes shot back.

"Ladies, can we just calm down a bit?" Lorraine tried to bring the group back into order.

It was the next day after Ben had been arrested and charged for murdering Eleanor. The whole town was talking about it.

Mom had called all the ladies over the following night after they heard how Ben had tried to kidnap me.

"I wish I had seen Tarzan take down Ben. I heard it was like something in the movies." Elizabeth took a sip of tea.

"Were you scared, Dove?" Weenie looked at me with big eyes.

"Yes. But I knew everything would work out. And it did."

"I'm shocked that Eleanor had a son and no one knew." Donna shook her head.

"Well, someone did know." Maggie grinned. "Lester knew. It was someone from Jackson. Lester was in the same military unit with him and he told him. That's one reason that Lester and Eleanor never got along."

"My goodness. You just never know about people." Mom shook her head.

"Well, I knew something was wrong with Ben," Lorraine stated.

"You did?" I asked.

"Yes. I always found it odd that he was always trying to get close to Eleanor. I mean the woman is as mean as they come. He would always defend her when someone said something bad about her. I think he has that same meanness deep in his soul that she had." Lorraine took a bite of a tea cake.

"I guess things will go back to normal now." Sylvia smiled.

"Not everything." Agnes shook her head. "Pastor John wants Peter to stay a bit longer at his home. He's already said he's going to fully fund his parents back in the mission field if they are willing to go."

"I think that's nice."

"That's not all that's changed. Seems like there's trouble in paradise between Dean and Samantha," Elizabeth stated. "I saw them arguing on the square as I was taking Petunia to the flower shop."

"What were they saying?" Weenie asked.

"I couldn't tell but I believe I heard a certain woman's name thrown into the conversation."

All eyes turned to me.

I held up my hand. "I have nothing to do with their relationship."

"Girl, you have everything to do with their relationship." Bertha snorted.

"That's right Dove. Dean's always been in love with you." Weenie smiled.

The room grew quiet until Petunia let out a burp from her dog bed in the corner. She lifted her head and walked over to me and bleated.

She nuzzled my hand.

"Look Dove. Even Petunia is jealous. She thinks you like Tarzan better than her." Elizabeth laughed.

I rubbed the goat under the chin. When I stopped she let out a bleat.

Everyone laughed.

"I can promise you, Petunia. No one will ever take your place as my favorite." I stood and went over to the whiteboard.

I picked up the eraser and cleared the suspects' names off the board.

I looked at everyone. "I feel kind of bad that I never suspected Ben."

"Don't honey. Men are like that. They play tricks on women's hearts. That's why when you find a good man you don't let him go." Mom looked at me.

I sighed. I knew she was talking about Dean. And I knew she was right.

"I have some news. I was contacted by a manufacturer in Los Angeles who asked me to send them some sketches of designs for women."

"Really, Dove? That's fantastic! Why didn't you say anything?" Weenie ran over and gave me a hug.

"Because I just sent off the drawings. I don't know if they want them or not. But it's a start."

"Heck yeah, it's a start." Agnes smiled.

I grabbed my teacup. "Why don't we end tonight with a toast?" Everyone grabbed their cups. I

I looked around the room at the ladies who already felt like family. It made me think of Ben and Peter.

Gratitude tugged in my heart. I cleared my throat. "To the best group of investigators and troublemakers I know."

Everyone toasted and laughed.

"But most of all, to my family."

# THE MYSTERY OF THE EXPLODING HEARTS QUILTS CHAPTER 1

It had been three weeks since I had heard from Dean. After solving the last murder in Harland Creek, he'd been asked to Tennessee to help with an investigation involving a missing college student.

Not that it bothered me. I mean, technically he was still dating Samantha and I was too busy helping my mom at her quilt shop to worry about some guy. The thing that bothered me the most was me dreaming about the last time Dean had kissed me. Images of his mouth on mine and his hands in my hair made my heart beat a little bit faster.

I groaned and quickened my steps to the doughnut shop. I needed my sugar fix and quick.

Just then the pharmacy door swung open and Samantha Vaughn stepped out. Startled at seeing me, her mouth dropped open.

"Hello, Samantha." I kept my voice polite and continued walking to my destination.

"Dove, wait."

My stomach dropped and I stopped. I wasn't in the mood

for this conversation. I was caffeine deprived and needed a jelly doughnut to stave off my lustful thoughts.

I turned and looked at the woman who' was now dating my ex-boyfriend. "Samantha, I really don't have time to talk. I have an appointment."

"It's important." She lifted her chin. "Besides, going to the doughnut shop doesn't classify as an appointment."

My face heated. "You should really stop keeping tabs on me. It's creepy."

"I'm sorry. It's just…" Her voice cracked.

"What? What is it?" I frowned.

"It's Dean. I didn't hear from him last night." She pressed her lips into a thin line.

I sighed heavily. "I'm sure he's just busy in Tennessee. It's not like he has to call every single night. Guys are notoriously bad about things like that."

She looked at me under my lashes. "Has he called you?"

I grimaced. "No. Why would he?"

She cocked her head. "Because I think something is wrong. Really, terribly wrong, Dove. I think Dean is in trouble."

# ABOUT THE AUTHOR

Jodi Allen Brice has written numerous books under a different pen name. Under Jodi Allen Brice she writes fiction and small town clean and sweet romance.

She transitioned away from paranormal romance in the year 2020 when the virus hit. She said she felt she needed to write a book that would change hearts and minds where Christ is concerned. She is a Christian who loves studying Bible prophesy and spending time with her family in Arkansas. She's is also an avid quilter and camping. Some-times she does both at the same time!

Check our her website at http://jodiallenbrice.com